The Fragrance of Rose

The Fragrance of Rose

Chirajit Paul

Srishti
PUBLISHERS & DISTRIBUTORS

Srishti Publishers & Distributors
Registered Office: N-16, C.R. Park
New Delhi – 110 019

Corporate Office: 212A, Peacock Lane
Shahpur Jat, New Delhi – 110 049
editorial@srishtipublishers.com

First published by
Srishti Publishers & Distributors in 2017

10 9 8 7 6 5 4 3 2 1

Printed and bound in India

I dedicate this novel to my dear wife Chayanika, without whose help it would not have been possible for me to capture a woman's perspective. I am also indebted to her (a media person in real life) for sharing knowledge on the media (and movie) industry, both of which served as vital backdrops. We have tried to give the story a realistic feel, now it is up to you to read and tell.

Prologue

Rinita Bose

Abhishek felt a vibration from under his pillow. He always kept his mobile on vibration mode while in bed. Being the manager of a project spread across half the globe, such vibrations were not uncommon. Almost ten out of thirty days a month, he was woken up by such midnight calls. Some critical business process in some country halfway across the hemisphere must have failed, started to fail or had been failing for some time. Though he could not recognize the caller, his sleepy brain was quick to realize it wasn't a work call as it flashed a local mobile phone number.

Abhishek picked up the phone, pulled himself out of bed, walked out into the verandah making as little noise as possible, lest his wife and child wake up. By the time he got into a position to accept the call, it got disconnected. Abhishek called back and heard a voice he had heard before, but could not place.

"Hello, this is Souvik. Chaitali's friend from RTC," said the male voice.

"Ah...Souvik! What is the matter...so late in the night?" asked Abhishek.

"Actually there is an emergency. Rinita is severely unwell. We are rushing her to the hospital."

"What happened?"

"Not sure. A local doctor is with us. Some gynecological trouble he said. We are taking her to Apollo."

"Okay, keep calm. Is Mahesh also with you?"

"Yes, he only contacted me."

"Okay, we will be there right away," said Abhishek and hung up.

Abhishek could hear the siren of the ambulance and occasional groaning from Rinita in the background. Rinita must have been in severe pain; she was not the kind who would let others know unless it was unbearable. Abhishek took a look at the time on his mobile – 2.30 a.m. He went up to Chaitali's side of the bed and gently shook her by her shoulders to wake her up. Once she was fully awake and aware of the situation, Chaitali was shivering, sweating and panicking.

In twenty minutes, Abhishek and Chaitali were heading at top speed towards Apollo hospital, leaving their two-year-old son under the watchful eyes of Chaitali's mother-in-law.

◆

Priyanshu was wide awake, lying on his bed, staring at the ceiling of his newly made up bedroom. A faint light came in from outside through the glass window. The shadow of the banyan tree leaves shivering in the cool breeze of a fading autumn created a moving pattern on Priyanshu's bedroom ceiling. His newly wedded wife sleeping in peace with her left hand on Priyanshu's chest did not know that even after six months of post-engagement courtship and fifteen days of marriage – which included seven days of honeymoon in Bali – Priyanshu was still not into her. At half past two in the morning, he was trying to find, in the moving pattern on the ceiling, the girl he wished was wearing the same wedding bangles his wife wore, and placing her hand on his chest the same way his wife did.

The phone kept on silent mode blinked from the bedside table and soon Priyanshu was behind the steering wheel of his 3 Series BMW, rushing towards Apollo. His newly wedded wife, in full oblivion and partial awakening, wished his sick friend a speedy recovery.

◆

Winter in Kolkata brings in a cool breeze at night, but in the hills of Darjeeling, it was already rather cold. In his home at the Wellington Tea Estate, fifteen kilometres downhill from Ghoom, Hemant Thapa was deep in sleep. He never had the necessity to lower the riger volume at night because his phone rang very rarely. Nobody in and around the sleepy town of Ghoom would ever make a phone call at that time unless it was absolutely necessary.

Hemant's phone rang at 2.45, and by 3.15, Chetri, the driver of the estate-owned Maruti Gypsy was turning on the ignition key, ready to head to Bagdogra airport where he would drop Hemant and return. Fortunately, he had not had any chang to drink that night, otherwise driving down the mountain trail through the dark would have been a risky affair.

◆

At three in the morning in his Mumbai home, Shahid Khan, like every night, was working on the script of his next movie. The glass ashtray on his study table fumed the last cigarette which had been stubbed recently. Immediately after the Kolkata call came in, he dialled the production team travel agency, requesting, in a non-negotiating tone, bookings in the first flight for Kolkata that morning.

Shahid walked out of the study, pushed the bedroom door gently and looked at his wife Fatima, sleeping like a baby. He returned to the study table, pulled out a piece of paper and wrote: *'Rose is seriously unwell, in hospital. I am taking the morning flight to Kolkata. Will call.'*

PART 1:
Chaitali Mukherjee and Souvik Halder

"Mine went further," said Rinita, looking at the ripples caused by the pebble she had thrown into the river. It was a summer afternoon, the between-tide time – when the water of the Ganga flowing through the flatland touching the banks of the Phoolbari village often looked so still as if it was in no hurry to culminate into the sea. Chaitali fiercely protested the claim while Mahesh, as always, presented a lost look.

After the initial disagreement, both Rinita and Chaitali turned to Mahesh for his decision. Mahesh always played the referee in such situations. Both Rinita and Chaitali granted him the privilege, knowing very well that autistic Mahesh could not deliver a fair judgment. Very often than not, a clueless Mahesh would pass his verdict in favour of Rinita, for whom he had a soft spot. Rinita would jump out of joy and plant a kiss on Mahesh's cheek every time he pronounced his predictable judgement. Chaitali, being more matured of the three, would shrug away the loss with a smile. The happiness of her two best friends was too precious to be sacrificed for a win at the silly games they played after school.

Mahesh sat with his legs drawn to his chest, resting against the wall of the century old Shiv temple on the banks of the river while Chaitali and Rinita sat facing the river, on the edge of the temple floor. They had collected a decent number of pebbles and took turns at throwing them into the river. With each throw either of them claimed to have surpassed the other in distance, and once the stock of pebbles exhausted, Mahesh got the holy role to play. To the surprise of both, Mahesh, for a change, announced Chaitali's name as the winner. Rinita, after overcoming the initial surprise, stretched out her arms to embrace Mahesh, kissed his cheek as always and said, "Still ... I love you dear." Mahesh blushed out of shyness while Chaitali smiled.

Chaitali, Rinita and Mahesh were childhood friends and neighbours at the Phoolbari village in the Hooghly district some fifty kilometres upstream the Ganga from Kolkata. They were of the same age group, but from diverse backgrounds. Chaitali came from a reputed and educated family – one of the most respected in Phoolbari. The joint family lived in a hundred-year-old huge palatial house which was known far and wide for organizing the most extravagant Durga Puja in the vicinity. In recent times, with the family growing and the income from family business receding, the extravagance had gone, but the annual ritual remained. Many family members had opted out of the family business and taken up jobs in Kolkata and elsewhere only to re-unite during the puja days. Chaitali's father, along with three more uncles, were still into the family business, trying hard to keep it afloat. Whether in business or in service, all her uncles were educated, cultured and modern.

Rinita's parents came and settled in Phoolbari after her father joined the Phoolbari Jute Mill as a head clerk. Her father was dark and strongly built, barely decent in terms of looks, and rather unpolished in social dealings, whereas her mother was fair and beautiful, and it appeared that she came from a more decent family than her spouse. The couple did not mingle much with the local people, neither did they have many friends or relatives visiting them. Evidently, their marriage did not seem to have received the blessings of their families. Few years after Rinita was born, the jute mill shut down, leaving her father and hundreds of other people jobless. While others took up jobs at other places, Rinita's father took to alcohol and gambling. Her mother took up babysitting jobs to run the household. Quarrels, fights and wife beating became regular in the family until four years later when her father passed away. Apparently he was beaten to death by a group of fellow drunkards. Rinita's mother was rather relieved than sad at her husband's sudden demise.

Mahesh's mother, after suffering heavily from severe jaundice at the time of pregnancy, had passed away during delivery. Doctors could not say with certainty whether it was the jaundice or malnutrition or any other thing that had caused autism in Mahesh. Mahesh's father, a worker in a local oil mill, was so hurt by the sudden loss of his beloved wife, that he sought solace in god. He started spending time at temples and in the company of sadhus, searching for something which was far, and ignoring the one thing which was near – his son and his disease. Mahesh, therefore, was sent to a regular school where he was subjected to mental and physical torture by the other 'normal' students, sometimes by some 'normal' teachers too. Mahesh's dropout, which was a matter of time, happened when he was in class eight.

◆

While they were still in their early teens, one afternoon on their way back from school, Rinita took Chaitali by her hand to the riverside temple to show her something 'confidential'.

"What is it?" Chaitali wanted to wrap it up fast. She did not want to face the long list of questions her mother would greet her with if she was late.

"Shhh," Rinita placed her index finger on her lips.

The naughty smile on her face suggested she had some mischief in mind. She placed her school bag on the ground, opened it and pulled out a thin book neatly wrapped in brown paper.

"What is it?" Chaitali asked again rather impatiently.

Rinita handed over the book to Chaitali who opened it and seeing some pictures in brown shut it immediately. Chaitali and

Rinita exchanged glances; the mischief of Rinita's face was prominent

Chaitali opened it again, this time after making sure nobody was around to notice what they were doing. The page she opened had some white naked couples in penetrated postures. Chaitali carefully turned few more pages.

"Where did you get this?" whispered Chaitali.

"Got it from a friend."

"Which friend?"

"You don't know all my friends, do you?"

Chaitali and Rinita went to the same school. They used to read in the same class till two years ago when Rinita flunked and stayed back in class six for one more term. They went to and returned from school together, also played the same games with the same group of girls during recess. Chaitali thought she knew all of Rinita's friends, but a direct challenge from Rinita put her on the back foot.

"See this, see this." Rinita pulled the book out of Chaitali's hand and turned to a page which she had kept folded around the edge and pointed at the size of the male organ of the model. Chaitali felt like throwing up at the sight of a giant size male organ with some white fluid dripping from it, which the female model was wiping off with her tongue. Taking her eyes away she said, "Are you mad?"

'Why? You don't like it? I am enjoying every bit of it," Rinita replied.

"Not at all." Though from the inside Chaitali felt a compulsive need, like any girl of her age, to gulp the rest of the pictures.

"Then give it back and go home, nice girl."

"I will definitely go home, but you get rid of this shit. It will land us in trouble."

"It will land me into trouble if it does, and I will make sure it won't." Rinita was upset with Chaitali's lack of enthusiasm.

"You didn't tell me where you got it from?" Chaitali asked again.

"None of your business, nice girl." Rinita's 'nice girl' was certainly a dig.

Rinita never shared the name of the friend, nor did she bring up that topic again. When Chaitali came to know about the real source, she was more worried than angry, realizing that Rinita was treading a dangerous line.

Chaitali and Rinita used to go to school and return together on Chaitali's bicycle. Every year during April and May, Chaitali had 'Rabindrasangeet' practice sessions after school. She happened to be the lead singer in the annual 'Rabindra Janmotsav' function held at the school. During those months Chaitali returned late from school, and Rinita used to return on her own, and sometimes with some like-minded friends.

Being extremely beautiful, she had set fire in the hearts of many boys. Many of them queued outside the school at the time when the school ended, to catch a glimpse of her. Chaitali generally kept Rinita well-guarded from the hungry intensions of those boys. But that one month when Rinita was alone, she was most vulnerable, also most free to further her fantasies.

One smart fellow kept following her for a few days, got a letter delivered through safe hands, and managed to get Rinita meet him at an inexpensive café near the railway station. There they met inside the close confines of a 'cabin' meant for families. Rinita's first touch of male skin, first kiss and first look at porn books all happened inside the café cabin. The boy had purchased the book from a roadside book stall in Kolkata's Esplanade area, which he was happy to gift Rinita in exchange of her physical generosity.

Rinita's one month of freedom ended and she never again made eye contact with the boy, who continued to stand opposite the school gate during school end time hoping to repeat the adventure.

◆

In the evenings Chaitali, Rinita and Mahesh used to play badminton in the corner of the park. The boys who played cricket in winter and football in summer had it in their routine to tease Mahesh for not playing the boy's game with them, and once their own game was over, to crowd around the badminton play area cheering a good smash or a good return. Some liked Chaitali for her intense, sharp and intelligent looks, while most liked Rinita for her more feminine beauty and occasional reciprocation to quick flirts.

Soumen, the leader of the boy's gang, slightly senior to the average boys, had a commanding personality, decent looks and immense leadership qualities. His father and Rinita's father were colleagues at the jute mill. Perhaps because of the parental connect, Soumen was rather protective of Rinita. Soumen studied science in college and acting under the direction of his father, was in constant touch with Rinita's mother, helping her with any problems she faced from time to time.

Once, when Rinita was in class nine, her mother expressed to Soumen, concern regarding her inattentive daughter's studies. Soumen did not think twice before offering to guide her in the science subjects.

Soumen coached Rinita three times a week in the evenings in her house. On most days, only the two of them used to be in the house with Rinita's mother out on her baby-sitting job.

Rinita was only too happy to have Soumen as her tutor. With the kind of looks, body, personality and leadership traits, Soumen was the man of her fantasy. Very often she imagined Soumen in place of the white male models in the pictures. Rinita knew the kind of body Soumen had; she had seen his bare body when the gang of boys went for a swim in the Ganga. Like a matching body, Soumen must have had an organ which matched the size and strength of the white models, she thought.

While Soumen tried his best to generate some interest for science in Rinita, her interest remained confined to finding out what Soumen thought about beautiful bollywood actresses, or the beautiful girls in Phoolbari, or in his college, and whether he had a girlfriend. Soumen answered some, dodged some and ignored some of the missiles thrown at him. The more he tried with science, the more Rinita got into such things.

One evening, during a power cut, with a lone candle throwing up as much light as was necessary to make a romantic setting, Soumen and Rinita sat face to face with trigonometry problems waiting to be solved. Soumen's shirt was wet with sweat and stuck to his perfectly shaped chest, and, instead of the mathematics book, Rinita's eyes were fixed on it. The intoxicating sweaty smell coming out of Soumen's body did something to Rinita which made her spring out of her chair, blow the candle off, hug Soumen hard with arms around his head, pressing her tight developing breasts against his face and murmur, "Soumen da, I cannot live without you."

Soumen fled as if he had seen a ghost, and never came back.

Chaitali stepped out of the studio after a marathon live session. A veteran one time superstar actor had joined politics – the need for making stories out of nothing to fill up the space for a 24X7 news channel was done with. She entered the make-up room for a quick correction of the make-up she had to put on before the show. She was in a hurry to rush to a colleague's wedding, and was already late. While the make-up artist executed her tone-down and touch-up instructions, Chaitali checked the inbox and missed call alerts on her mobile phone.

'The lipstick on the upper lip has smeared out a bit, otherwise looking stunning,' read a message from Arindam Mukherjee, the

Editor-in-Chief, Chaitali's second upline, the undisputed boss at RTC News.

Chaitali quickly checked her lips in the large mirror in front of her and found that the lipstick had obediently remained behind the boundary drawn on her perfectly shaped lips.

"What does this mean?" Chaitali showed the message to the middle-aged lady doing the make-up, curious to understand the smearing logic. Chaitali had a habit of wiping her face with a handkerchief every now and then, but that was before she joined RTC News as a trainee news anchor. Ever since, she used scented moist tissues for the purpose and substituted brushing motion with tapping.

"Ignore such messages," replied Swapna aunty. Swapna Roy, the make-up artist was a loving aunty for all the juniors who turned to her for advice on almost all personal and professional matters. Mrs. Roy, a widow and mother of two, was a veteran in the industry and had known all the bulls and bears inside out.

"But what does it mean?" Chaitali reapeated.

"You don't have to know everything. Just remember, never reply to such messages and never offer any indulgence," was the stern reply. Evidently, Swapna aunty was not ready to discuss more on the topic. An intelligent Chaitali got the hint – that she'd have to figure it out herself.

Souvik was driving Chaitali and two other colleagues to the wedding in his car. Chaitali, looking for an opportunity to discuss the matter with him – her most trusted friend in office – whispered into Souvik's ear from the non-driver's seat, "Need to discuss something in private."

Souvik nodded.

The parking lot was away from the entrance. Chaitali accompanied Souvik while the others off-boarded at the gate.

"Can you tell me what this means?" Chaitali showed Souvik the message.

Souvik took a look at the message, and said, "Nothing serious, just ignore it."

He opened the door in an attempt to step out, indicating that he wanted to cut short the conversation, but Chaitali held his hand.

"Don't run away, explain to me what this means," she said.

"It means," Souvik answered unwillingly, "that he is trying to figure out whether you are game."

"Game?" Chaitali was clueless.

"Whether you are willing to...compromise." Souvik hesitated but at the same time realized that beating around the bush wouldn't help.

"Compromise?"

"He is a lecher. The rest you can understand on your own." Souvik dashed out of the car and waited outside, looking away from a shocked Chaitali.

Chaitali soon overcame the initial disbelief, emerged out of the car and threw another difficult question at Souvik.

"And you are his right hand man, at work... and I presume, at pleasure as well." Chaitali's attack was too direct, but Souvik managed to keep his cool.

"I do not endorse all that he does, or all that I see...but I have a job to keep, a family to feed, and you know pretty well it is a small industry with limited opportunities."

"Do you supply girls to him?"

"Come on Chaitali, this is too much."

"You are his right hand man...you know all his secrets...and you are claiming sainthood?"

"I am not claiming sainthood," Souvik tried to explain his position which had become undoubtedly precarious. "Yes, I had to stand as his alibi on one or two occasions when he got caught by his wife...and sometimes I...I...arrange the logistics," stammered Souvik out of shame of being unmasked.

"Get me a taxi, I want to go home."

"Come on Chaitali, we are here for the wedding."

"I don't care, I am feeling sick…get me a taxi, will you? If not, I will manage on my own." A desperate Chaitali started walking towards the main road. Souvik followed her, got her a yellow cab and returned to the wedding.

❦

Chaitali passed both her board examinations, tenth and twelfth with flying colours, did her graduation with major in Economics from Presidency College and obtained a Master's degree in Mass Communication from Jadavpur University. She was picked up directly from campus by the number one Bengali news channel Round-The-Clock News, popularly known as RTC News, as a trainee.

Rinita, having flunked again in class nine, managed to scrape through the tenth and twelfth, and after her mother passed away just before the twelfth board examinations, she gave up further studies and took up a receptionist's job in a doctor's clinic in Hooghly town. Dropping out from further studies, for her, was a mix of survival compulsion as well as exercise of choice. Her studies were squarely because of her mother's insistence. Once she was free from the obligation, she opted out from what she never liked doing.

But after two years, Rinita realized that the boring job wasn't taking her anywhere. The money was not great, nor was there a promising future. Her job had become another trigonometry class, she thought. Watching Chaitali prepare for her third year examinations, a positive envy crawled into her mind. She realized she needed a graduation degree if she hoped to do anything better. Within a year of sharing her desire with Chaitali, Rinita had a B.A degree suffixing her name on the curriculum vitae from a lesser known private university in Andhra Pradesh, which conferred degrees on correspondence.

Within six months of getting into RTC, Chaitali had built a reputation for herself – of being smart, with an acute sense of news. She got into the good books of the senior management, including Arindam, and enjoyed, much to the envy of the seasoned and senior anchors, all the good shows, prime shifts, and challenging assignments. Soon Chaitali became a permanent fix at the 'News at Nine', the maximum TRP show at RTC.

While she consolidated her position, Chaitali did a few things for her childhood friends as well. She got Mahesh a peon's job at RTC, and exploiting her channel contacts, secured concessions from the best photographer in town for Rinita's portfolio.

Rinita always wanted to be an actress and a glossy portfolio was the first definitive step. Chaitali took into her hands the responsibility of shaping Rinita's career. She thought, with the kind of looks Rinita had, the portfolio would definitely generate a certain amount of interest among people to whom dull beauty was not a bad thing. And to cash upon the opportunities Rinita would be required to stay in Kolkata. Surviving in Kolkata without a stable job wasn't an easy thing, and therefore, Chaitali arranged a training-cum-trainee's job for Rinita at Shekhar's, a premier beauty parlour chain.

Rinita had a difficult dream to chase, which, to some extent seemed to find some direction with her shifting base to Kolkata.

Mahesh also settled down in his new job. At RTC, being Chaitali's friend earned him special status. Nobody dared to laugh at him or crack a joke like they would have done ordinarily when Mahesh unnecessarily arranged things in order or hung on to the last words of others in a conversation, repeating them in a murmur.

Phoolbari village for all the three had become a thing of the past.

◆

Unlike trigonometry, Rinita proved to be a fast learner in things of beauty. She picked up the tricks of creating a marvel of beauty out of an ordinary structure – the hair dressing, modern or traditional, to suit the shape of the face or the structure of the body, the shape of the nail tip that would be in perfect harmony with the fingers, the colour of the nail enamel which would go with the personality or the occasion, the nude or loud make-up style that would match up to the taste of the customer were things she had learnt in practically no time.

"She has a flair for the beauty business," Shekhar once told Chaitali when she enquired how Rinita was doing.

Rinita, on her off days, paid visits to big and small advertisement agencies with hard and soft copies of her portfolio. While most of them would collect the soft copies and dump them in crowded folders bursting with similar 'jpeg' files from numerous aspiring young models, others would offer free advice along with machine made semi cold coffee, that she should compete for beauty pageants. "Winning a pageant gives maximum exposure," they said.

Her first break in the modeling world came through the very photographer who had clicked her portfolio – a still for a newspaper advertisement for a cotton printed sari. The very moderately budgeted ad-campaign was on the lookout of a new, inexpensive face that would be good enough to carry the rather dull looking cotton saris they manufactured.

The entire amount Rinita earned out of her cotton sari venture was spent in one evening, in a lavish dinner thrown at a five star hotel attended by her two best friends, Chaitali and Mahesh.

"Why do you have to spend so much?" asked Chaitali in a whisper lest the guests at the other tables heard her.

"Why not dear? Both of you mean so much to me. Who else do I have?"

"That's fine dear, but burning all your hard earned money is not wise."

"It is not burning money dear; it is a humble way to thank you…to say how much I love you."

"I love you too but …."

"I love you too," said Mahesh cutting into Chaitali.

Both Rinita and Chaitali turned to Mahesh and found that he was tapping the table with his fork.

Rinita held his hand to stop the tapping and said in a sweet tone as if she was talking to a child, "I love you too Mahesh, we all love each other."

"But you don't do anything for me…Chaitali has given me a job."

"What can I do for you dear?"

"Marry me." Mahesh looked up to meet Rinita's eyes, chuckled and blushed.

"Of course dear, one day I will definitely marry you." Rinita knew how to tackle Mahesh. She had been doing it for years.

Chaitali's super boss Arindam, known for his astounding diligence in all his pursuits, relentlessly kept on trying to dupe Chaitali to his bed, until one day, he found a wedding invitation on his desk – Chaitali was getting married to a foreign educated MBA working with a multinational consulting firm as a strategy consultant.

Arindam got infuriated at his defeat, tore apart the wedding card and swore to teach Chaitali the lesson of her life.

"I will teach her the lesson of her life…she will remember whom she has dealt with, Arindam told Souvik in a state of high degree intoxication.

"Leave it Arindam da, you know she is not like the other girls," Souvik tried to underplay the gravity with which Arindam perceived the matter.

"What do you mean she is not like the other girls?" Arindam was loud.

Souvik wanted to say that Chaitali was too smart for the like of Arindam, but since he had a job to save and a family to run, what he actually said was, "She is not good enough for you. You've had top models and film stars (read, struggling starlets in search of fame) warming your bed. She is such an ordinary girl."

"Correct...I have brought to my bed whoever I desired. Nobody ever had the courage to say no to me." Arindam's ego had certainly been hurt.

"I am the boss of this place!" shouted Arindam without realizing that he was sitting in a bar and not in his office.

"Yes-yes, be calm, you are definitely the boss of RTC," Souvik pointed out the correction so that the next time he shouted, the bar owner wouldn't panic to recheck his title.

"Correct...I am the boss of RTC...I can make or break the lives of my employees...I will break her and she will have to repent... she will fall at my feet and beg for mercy..." Arindam continued at the top of his voice. The drunkards from the nearby tables had some free entertainment. Being in the media business, Arindam was a known face. A tipsy celebrity stepping on garbage was a natural source of fun for anybody.

"Yes-yes...sure-sure...let us go now," said Souvik fearing that the owner might call in the bouncers anytime.

"I will...I will..." Arindam's face banged against the table; before he could explain his conviction, he fell unconscious.

◆

The sprawling lawn of the five start hotel was studded with guests – friends, relations, acquaintances, and colleagues from both sides.

Chaitali's side of the guest list boasted of celebrities: movie stars, sports persons, political leaders.

Had there been a concept of bridesmaid in Hindu marriages, Rinita would have definitely been called one. She was omnipresent all throughout the four day long celebration comprising rituals, fun and parties. On the reception day, she was on the stage helping the bride manage the gifts. Beside her sincere helping effort, she lost no opportunity to get photographed with the guests who mattered. Chaitali, noticing her enthusiasm, introduced Rinita to all those she thought could be, even remotely, of some help to her.

Rinita, looking stunning as usual in a navy blue and gold handwoven Kanjivaram saree and matching kundan jewellery caught both Souvik and Arindam's attention without much effort. Souvik and Rinita exchanged words and business cards whereas Arindam, while obliging photo hungry guests kept an eye on the beautiful lady from a distance. His lustful eyes roamed around each and every part of Rinita's body whether covered or exposed. The oval shaped face had a pointed chin and slightly raised cheek bones; the round black eyes were darkened with mascara and had long eye lashes; the lips tapering gradually at the sides wore a natural matte lipstick. The medium length black hair cut in layers with slightly left-of-the-center parting and locks falling down both sides of the face making it look longer than it actually was.

The party got over and the made-for-each-other couple flew off to Spain for their honeymoon. Souvik called up Rinita and wasted no time asking her whether she was interested in a media job.

"What kind of job?" asked a surprised Rinita.

"The kind Chaitali does."

"Oh-no. News anchoring is a difficult job. I know how hard Chaitali works. I neither have the education, nor the inclination," she confessed.

"She has a gift, yes, but that doesn't mean that others who aren't as natural as her aren't doing well in this business. Anything can be learnt, you see." It did not matter whether Souvik himself believed in what he said, but as it was his boss's wish and he had to save his job, he had to convince Rinita.

"No, but still…"

"And think about the salary." Souvik released the most powerful weapon he had in store.

"Okay but…"

"Why so many 'buts'? I am there to train you. Your best friend Chaitali is there to train you."

Rinita did not get a chance to consult her best friend who was in Spain before accepting the tempting offer that required her to join with immediate effect.

Chaitali returned from a happy honeymoon to find that her prime time slots were lost, and lost to none other than her best friend.

A naïve Rinita gave a big hug to Chaitali on her return thinking that she would be happy to see her at RTC, without realizing that she had become a pawn in a nasty plan.

In her mailbox, Chaitali found a three-line mail communication from Arindam: 'The prime time slots from now onwards will be anchored by our new recruit Rinita Bose. You are required to take charge of the daily breakfast show. As an additional responsibility, you are required to oversee Rinita's grooming as an anchor.'

"What is going on?" Chaitali called Souvik.

"Don't tell me you didn't expect Arindam to hit back," Souvik said shattering her expectation of solidarity.

"But this is hitting below the belt. Why is he dragging Rinita into this?"

"I am helpless Chaitali...I am only carrying out orders. You are my good friend and you know my compulsions."

Chaitali disconnected the call. She knew Souvik was spineless and Arindam had hit where it hurt most. The breakfast show did not have much audience. The shift from prime time to breakfast show was a sharp demotion. She decided to be patient and wait for her turn.

Chaitali's turn came, rather unexpectedly, within three months – Abhishek was allotted a five-year assignment in London and Chaitali decided to quit her job and accompany her better half. She was happy she could return a fitting reply to Arindam, and Arindam, though unhappy about the punishment plan failing, was happy to get rid of a disobedient, uncompromising employee.

Till the time Chaitali left for London, she, as a thorough professional, continued to host the morning show and train Rinita into a news anchor's role to the best of her mind's acceptance.

Both Rinita and Mahesh were happy for Chaitali and went to the airport to see her off. Neither of them realized the real game being played in the background to inflict pain on her.

◆

Round-The-Clock News without Chaitali became a happy hunting ground for Arindam who had his eyes fixed on Rinita. It was difficult for Rinita after the fantastic offer dropping into her lap right out of the blue, to resist any proposal from the super boss, unless it was nakedly obscene. Thus, one day, when Arindam asked her whether she would accompany him to watch the famous Bengali play 'Raktakarabi', she could find no reason to say no. His wife had suddenly fallen sick and could not turn up was the reason given to Rinita by Arindam, which again Rinita had no reason not to believe.

Inside the theatre, Arindam put his hand on Rinita's hand a couple of times on the pretext of using the common armrest. Often, he took his face close to Rinita's ear to explain the nuances of the intellectually rich play, in the process taking a careful look at the cleavage protruding out of the tight breast-wear lying under an almost transparent white chiffon saree. Rinita had no reasons to believe any of these were intentional.

Rinita started winning frequent invitations to join Souvik and Arindam over a drink, initially at hotels and restaurants and eventually at Arindam's spare flat on the outskirts of the city. The apartment which had minimal decoration, according to Arindam, was purchased for investment purpose, though in reality it was used to venue Arindam's sexual escapades. Rinita took pride in such invitations, partly because of the coveted company and partly because the irk they brought to the faces of the other fellow anchors, all of whom for some unknown reason always behaved rudely with her.

On every occasion, after a couple of drinks, Souvik would get a call or encounter a crisis work situation and would take his leave, leaving Arindam and Rinita in the middle of some intense discussion – the subject of which could be matters of grave importance or at times matters of utter silliness.

Arindam talked amongst other things, about the emptiness of his life: about some chronic illness of his wife, hinting at times at an unsatisfactory sex life, about how much he liked children but god had not granted him one, about how jittery and ill tempered his wife had become due to the prolonged ailment and medication, and how peace and happiness from his life had evaporated.

Souvik nodded, sometimes offered a comment or two in an effort to add more authenticity to the story.

Rinita listened to the stories with full attention and moist eyes, believing them to be true.

After almost two months of continuous effort, Arindam thought the fruit had become ripe enough to be plucked and consumed.

As per plan, one day, Arindam remained out of office, and his phone had remained switched-off. Souvik, offering a tensed look told Rinita that Arindam's wife was seriously ill and was admitted in a hospital. Souvik asked her not to discuss the matter with anybody in office as Arindam did not like discussing personal matters with colleagues – "Discussing personal matters was like exposing your vulnerability to the world and it doesn't befit leaders," he said was what Arindam believed. They planned to visit the hospital in the evening.

When the time came, Souvik and Rinita left for the hospital in Souvik's car. Souvik took a longer route than usual and by the time they reached the hospital gate, visiting hours was almost over. Souvik dropped Rinita at the main entrance and took his car to the parking lot. By the time Souvik rejoined Rinita at the entrance and headed inside, they saw Arindam coming out. He looked tired, as if he had not slept for days, and sad with unkempt hair and unshaved beard, very unlike an otherwise well-dressed and well-maintained Arindam.

Arindam, walking absentmindedly out of the gate, did not notice the two of them.

"How is she now?" Souvik asked. Genuine concern could be felt coming out of the words.

"Oh, you two are here. But visiting hours have just ended. She is still in intensive care." Arindam sounded hopelessly depressed.

"What happened to her, Arindam da?" asked Rinita.

Only Rinita's portion of the drama was unscripted and therefore, whenever Rinita asked a question, no matter how innocent or harmless it was, there would be an unusual pause, Arindam and Souvik would exchange glances, and either of them would come up with an extempored reply to manage the situation.

"Leave it Rinita, it is a complicated mental condition. I am too tired to talk about all this now. I need to get back home and rest," said Arindam offering a mixed expression of irritation, disgust and sorrow.

Rinita had tried asking the name of the disease a few times, but never succeeded in securing a straight answer. The kind of replies she obtained were: "What will you do with the details, you are not a medical expert", "Even the best known experts are failing to cure her. It will only make you sad" or "It is a serious state of melancholy. Not being able to bear a child can have very serious psychological reactions, you see."

"Yes, you look tired. You seriously need to take some rest, may be catch up with some sleep." Rinita sympathized with Arindam's stressed condition.

Rinita's words alerted Arindam that looking too serious could spill water on his dreams. So he promptly changed his pitch and said, "Going back home will not rid me of the pain...she is everywhere in that house and anything I see or touch would remind me of her...I need to divert my mind from her thoughts."

"Then let's go to the other flat," said Souvik, promptly playing a perfect devil's accomplice. "We cannot leave him alone in this condition, can we?" he said turning to Rinita.

"Oh definitely not," was the anticipated reply. Rinita did not notice when the two men smiled and winked at each other.

In less than an hour, the three of them were comfortably grounded on the heavily cushioned sofa in the living room of Arindam's flat, clinking their glasses, wishing for the speedy recovery of Arindam's falsely sick wife.

After two pegs of vintage scotch, Arindam headed for the washroom and Souvik received a phone call informing him of some news item which would require his urgent attendance in office. Souvik had to rush, leaving Rinita in the safe hands of Arindam.

Two more rounds and Arindam was sitting on the floor close to Rinita's feet, blaming the poor formation of the starts for the insurmountable sorrow inflicted upon him.

Alcohol and emotion have traditionally been a fatal combination. Rinita, already under the significant influence of alcohol was precariously standing at the edge of the cliff, waiting to be pushed.

Suddenly Arindam started weeping; Rinita could not help it, and held his head with both hands and pressed it close against her lap. The golden moment for which Arindam had waited and planned meticulously had come. He gradually pushed his head further inside Rinita's lap between her legs, stretched his hands around her waist in a hug, and with his face dug into Rinita's lap, continued weeping more intensely.

Rinita brushed her soft long fingers through his head for some time, forming rings with his hair. She dipped her head to bring it closer to Arindam's and rested her chin on his head. Arindam lifted this head to directly look into Rinita's eyes, released his arms from the embrace of the hips and with his right hand touched her face gingerly. Arindam waited for some time to study Rinita's reaction at his sudden advances. Rinita continued to look into Arindam's eyes without offering any repulsion. Arindam touched her lips with his index finger, rolled his finger over her soft moist lower lip. Rinita's lips parted in excitement. Arindam gathered more courage from what he understood as indulgence and rose from the ground to sit on the cushion beside Rinita and rested his lips gently on hers. Rinita shut her eyes and started licking his lips. Arindam lifted his left hand, pulled away the dupatta to expose a lot of skin around the breast area, and placed it gently on Rinita's right breast from over the skin tight kurti she had worn. With both her lips and breasts compromised, Rinita's excitement started rising. She wrapped her arms around Arindam's and held him tightly, locked her lips against his. Arindam gathered more courage, unbuttoned the top few buttons of her dress and slipped his left hand inside the laced bra. Arindam's fingers brushed against her nipples and the lip lock became firmer with tongues clashing against each other with lightning frequency.

While the lips ensured their contribution, and Arindam's hand had already cupped Rinita's tight little thing, Rinita's hands groped a thing slightly lower. Her hands touched Arindam's thigh and moved upwards until the zip of his trousers could be felt. Rinita used both her hands to untie the belt, unbutton the hook, and rip apart the chain. She touched the naked tip once and started stroking the big thing with her hand.

Arindam felt a shiver when Rinita's skin touched the tip.

The stroking got more vigorous with time and excitement, and Arindam had to put a stop to it. The last thing he wanted was an oral climax. He forcefully but kindly removed Rinita's hand, relaxed the kiss and stood up. The skin on the surface had rolled backto make way for the swollen meat creating a bigger tip circumference. Arindam applied force to pull Rinita to a standing position. Rinita was under the influence of vintage scotch, and could not stand erect. Arindam lifted her with both arms as if he was lifting his newly wedded wife to bed, and with unsteady steps went into the bedroom. The alcohol had taken full effect on Rinita; she barely retained her senses. She had no strength to stand on her feet or offer any resistance to what she might or might not have approved.

Arindam dropped her on the bed. Rinita could hardly keep her eyes open. She murmured something, which an equally intoxicated Arindam could not understand, nor did he care. He ripped her kurti apart, pulled off the already out of place bra and leggings, undressed himself, forcefully stretched out her legs and pushed inside.

He stroked for five minutes to satisfaction, sprayed white fluid all over Rinita's body, lifted himself from her body which had fallen out of senses and lay flat on the bed besides her, panting heavily. All this while, Rinita lay like a corpse, she offered no particular expression of joy or pain.

❧

Rinita opened her eyes; her eyelids still heavy from the effects of alcohol. She could see a white wide wall and a ceiling fan rotating at moderate speed. It was the ceiling of a room she had not known previously. Rinita took some time to acclimatize to the situation. She felt a severe headache. She took some time to realize it wasn't her bedroom. She sat up on the bed. The sheet slipped down to rest folded around her waistline. Rinita could see her naked body outside the sheet. She cupped her breasts in a spontaneous reaction, crossing her arms across each other. She looked around the room carefully, but could not figure out where she was. One could make out that it was daytime, but what time of the day it was, was impossible to tell as heavy curtains blocked the sunlight from venturing freely inside the room. Rinita rolled her eyes around the room.

Once she was sure that there was nobody else in the room who could see her in that condition, and that the door and windows were firmly shut, Rinita dropped her feet on the ground and wrapped herself in the white sheet. She noticed the only piece of her own belonging which she was still wearing was her wrist watch which showed 10.30.

The moment she rested her full body weight on her legs, she felt an ache all over her body, as if somebody has beaten her up, with an especially severe pain in the vaginal area.

Rinita could not figure out what had happened and how; the headache did not help much in recollecting the happenings of the previous night.

Rinita reached the dressing table and stood in front of the full size mirror. Her face looked tired, bindi smeared across her brow, hair untied and out of place. She dropped her eyes gradually down her body still wrapped in the white sheet and noticed red spots, small and larger than small around the lower portion of the sheet. Her eyes caught sight of a bouquet of red roses and a packet wrapped in beautiful gift paper placed on the flat surface of the dressing table.

Rinita lifted the bouquet and found a card placed between two beautiful roses – 'Thank you for everything – Arindam' written in blue ink. Rinita picked up the packet and unwrapped it. An expensive kurti lay in the box. Rinita placed both the top-wear and the flowers back on the table. The pain in her private areas felt unbearable. She unwrapped the sheet to expose her fully bare body before the mirror. The sheet settled in a circle on the ground around her feet. Rinita glanced through her naked body from the top towards the bottom. Her eyes got stuck at a bite mark on the lower portion of her left breast just above the nipple along the circumference of the areola. The mark clearly caused by uncontrolled teeth-work had caused a deep injury; the area had turned bluish black. She ran her fingers gently over the bruised area only to feel a burning sensation. Her eyes then reached the private area. She placed her middle finger on the vaginal split. Her hand wetted in blood. She noticed dried out blood around the inside portion of her thigh. She lost very little time in realizing that her virginity was lost.

Rinita got out of the bedroom into the living room to find an empty bottle of expensive whisky, toppled glasses, and the torn kurti she had worn the previous evening neatly folded and placed on the center table. Her bra, panty, dupatta and leggings she had worn were also folded and kept under the kurti. Very neat job, she thought. There was no reason why Rinita would still not remember how and why she was there in that condition.

Rinita picked up her belongings, went to the washroom and had a long bath. She brushed herself fiercely in some kind of anger and frustration. She dressed herself, wearing the new kurti unwillingly, as her own was torn. She picked up her purse, mobile phone which did not work because of a charge drain-out and walked out of the flat and the building, taking a taxi straight to office. She had a bulletin to catch at 1.00 p.m.

The bouquet of roses remained where they were.

What a meticulously planned trap she had fallen prey to, Rinita thought resting against the back seat of the taxi, rushing towards the RTC News building. She wanted to stop at a shopping mall and buy another top, but there was no time.

In office, Rinita walked past Arindam's glass cubicle straight to the make-up room. She noticed Arindam, who was having a meeting with the production team, watching her walk across the floor towards the make-up room. Rinita didn't care to look at him, neither at Souvik who was, like Arindam, following her actions from a safe distance. Both Arindam and Souvik took solace from the dress she was wearing. Rinita did the bulletin with usual ease, without letting anybody sense that something so horrible had happened to her.

At the end of the bulletin, Rinita left office and headed home. She had to have another bath with her own set of toiletries. Under the shower, she started scrubbing her body again, this time more vigorously. The anger, frustration and a sense of defeat of falling prey to unscrupulous designs revolved in her mind. The more the thoughts circled in her mind, the more forcefully she scrubbed herself. The loss of her virginity was never a concern for Rinita, she never had inhibitions about her body, but she wanted to gift her virginity to the man she would love. She wanted to enjoy, in equal measure as her lover the celebration of physicality, the pains and pleasure of the maiden venture into the delightful world of sexuality.

The sense of being looted off what she dreamt of offering as a gift pained her. She broke down into tears, tears which immediately got washed away in the shower. She rested against the wall and gradually slipped down into a sitting posture with her back against the wall and her legs drawn up close to her chest, like how Mahesh used to sit in the temple while she and Chaitali would throw stones far into the river, both claiming to have thrown farther. She stuck her head between her legs, wrapped her knees with her arms and kept weeping under the running water.

◆

The next day after office, Rinita invited Mahesh for a movie and dinner. Mahesh's company would keep her away from unwanted thoughts, she knew. Rinita, since her teenage years, had been fond of Bollywood movies. The world of unreal fantasies had kept her hopeful of better things in life – hope she never found in her humble background and bleak family condition. Rinita believed in the rags to riches stories, the poetic justices and the fairy tale endings. The hope that something magical could happen anytime to anybody kept her afloat throughout her life, against all odds.

They went for a romantic movie featuring a new pair of lead actors. The first half went rather well. During the interval, Mahesh volunteered to get popcorn. By the time he returned the second half had already begun. Somehow he groped his way to his seat. By the time he was back, the hero was proposing to his girl in a movie theatre, while watching a movie, with a tub of popcorn in his hand offering her some out of it – a setting exactly same as them and many others at the theatre. Rinita was on the edge of her seat engrossed into the scene when Mahesh, taking a clue from what he saw, while offering Rinita a share from the tub of popcorn, repeated in a soft voice, the dialogue he had just heard, "Will you marry me?" Rinita's attention broke, she looked at Mahesh. The innocence of Mahesh was in sharp contrast to what Rinita had experienced in recent times. Her eyes moistened but she controlled her emotions well in time and did what she did every time Mahesh did something similar. "Of course I will dear," she said while brushing his hair with her hand.

◆

Over the next few days, Rinita remained virtually on her own, with neither Souvik nor Arindam venturing close to her. She had very few friends in office. The other fellow anchors were envious of her recent closeness with Arindam, whereas her other colleagues had known Chaitali for years and had seen how unceremoniously she got marginalized by Arindam for getting married and her place being granted to Rinita. They blamed Rinita for Chaitali's sudden departure.

Rinita spent more time with Mahesh than ever before. Chaitali called her from London as she did from time to time, but Rinita could not make herself discuss the matter with her.

After almost a week's time, Souvik gathered some courage to say 'hello' to Rinita while crossing each other in the news room. Rinita in a split second debated in her mind whether she should respond or not. She returned it with a cold 'hi'. Souvik derived some courage out of the coldness and the next day, in the pantry, finding her alone, came up to her from behind and patted on her back. Rinita, though reluctantly, offered him the seat next to her. For some time, neither of them knew what to say.

"How many times have you done this in the past?" Rinita initiated the conversation. Souvik was taken aback.

"Done what?"

"What you did to me that night."

"He told me he was in love with you and wanted to propose to you that evening. He asked me to get a bouquet of flowers and a dress which I delivered to his house."

"So you did not know that he was planning to fuck me," Rinita said in a tone strong but low in volume, almost a whisper.

The 'f' word came as a shocker to Souvik. He had been an alibi to Arindam in several of his misdeeds, but had never faced such a direct charge from the victim. He remained silent with his head fallen.

"I am still waiting for your answer," Rinita got restless.

"I thought it would happen with consent."

"So you know that it has not happened with consent. He raped me."

Souvik remained silent.

"I demand an answer," Rinita raised her voice.

"He told me later that he had drugged you."

"Drugged me?"

"He mixed it in your drink."

"What kind of drug is it?"

"It instantly raises one's sexual urge."

"And then?"

"And then...it becomes consensual."

"I see...very wise."

Rinita paused for a moment and said, "Do you know I can go to the police?"

"I know you can...but it will be futile...he is very powerful. They will not register any complaint against him."

"Oh great!" Rinita exclaimed in despair.

"But I will advise you to talk to him...he is repeatedly insisting that he is in love with you. He has slept with many women in the past, but never looked back...never spoke of love...but in your case he is repeatedly talking of love."

"Tell me something, is his wife really sick?" Rinita pretended as if she had not heard what Souvik had just said.

"His wife is melancholic...but the hospital story was made up."

"I thought so."

"They do not stay together any longer."

"It is not possible for any sane woman to stay with a man like him."

Both remained silent for some time until Souvik said, "I will have to get back to work."

Rinita also joined him. Midway on the staircase, with no-body in the vicinity, Souvik said, "I am really sorry for what happened... but you please talk to him...he is dying to talk to you."

Rinita looked at Souvik and said, "You know what you deserve?" and before Souvik could guess an answer, Rinita slapped him hard. The sound echoed against the walls of the staircase. Souvik felt his left cheek with his left hand and watched Rinita walk down the stairs hitting the floor with her high wooden heels.

The next morning, Rinita was woken up by a knock on the door. At such time, she didn't expect anybody or anything other than the newspaper and milk which were left on her doorstep. Rinita, with sleepy eyes and irritated mood answered the door. A flower delivery man was standing with a big size bouquet of red roses in his hand. A white card could be seen stuck between two fully blossomed flowers.

"What?" asked Rinita knowing very well what it was.

"Delivery for you, madam."

"From whom?"

"Not sure madam...must be mentioned in the card."

Rinita picked up the card – 'Neither sorry nor love are good enough words to express what I am feeling' was written inside carrying the initials A.M. Rinita knew who A.M. was. She accepted the delivery and waited at the door until the delivery man walked till the end of the long corridor and down the steps. Once he was out of sight, she smashed the bouquet against the wall opposite her door. The bouquet was thrown with such force that it came apart and the beautiful flowers rolled over all around the place. Rinita banged the door behind her in anger.

In office, Arindam continued with his curious-but-careful approach, and Souvik maintained a safe distance from Rinita. Rinita conducted her business as usual and left. She did not want to spend even one moment more than what was expected of her in terms of working hours as agreed through the printed words of the offer letter. She preferred and rather enjoyed spending time with Mahesh, shopping or watching movies or going for long walks.

The following morning, the delivery man was back with a bouquet of red roses arranged in a different pattern. Rinita accepted the delivery and did exactly what she had done the previous day.

When the delivery man was about the knock Rinita's door on the third consecutive day, he saw a hand written note stuck with cello tape on the door which read 'The resident of this apartment is allergic to flowers. All are requested to co-operate for her well being. Thanks.' The delivery man placed the bouquet outside Rinita's door and walked away without knocking.

Besides Mahesh, the next best friend Rinita had in office was Mr Gupta, the cafeteria man. Cafeteria was one of the three places Rinita spent most of her office time in, the other two being the studio and the make-up room. Whenever she was free or done with her bulletin for the day, she visited the cafeteria. There she used to sit alone, for hours, watching the news or sport or movies on the wall-mounted TV with steaming coffee in her hands. In the initial days, she never exchanged more words with Mr Gupta than what was necessary to buy coffee. But gradually, both of them grew rather comfortable with each other and exchanged words beyond coffee or muffins or pastries.

The man who was in his early fifties had a daughter three years younger to Rinita. But that was not the only reason why he liked her. He liked the sweetness and kindness with which Rinita conducted herself with people much below her in the social chain, something which was a rare quality with youngsters in modern times. And Rinita found some parental affection in a place where most people were either unfriendly or malafidely friendly towards her.

From the old man, Rinita came to know about the history of the company and Arindam Mukherjee: how the channel, days before going live was poached by a rival upcoming group and lost more than fifty percent of its workforce, how Arindam set up a new team overnight, persuaded his people to work for more hours than what was humanly possible and delivered an on-air on the stipulated date, how he was rewarded by the management for his magnificent achievement with the top post and how Arindam, enjoying absolute power, evolved into a dictator and womanizer.

"He never let any attractive girl working here live in peace until she agreed to warm his bed," said the old man hesitantly. "Those who did compromise grew fast within the company until Arindam lost interest in them. A few like Chaitali who didn't oblige were demoted to unimportant job roles and heckled until they could not work here any longer."

The more Rinita heard about Arindam, her head burnt with anger, especially at the reference of Chaitali. Chaitali's reason of quitting the job, as known to the world, was different from what she had learnt that day.

"Even the men do not bring their beautiful wives to office parties, lest Arindam catches fancy," he said.

"Then why don't people protest?" Rinita asked an innocent question.

"Do you know how many people lost their jobs because they disapproved of what Arindam did?"

"The girls never went to the police?"

The old man smiled at the naïve question. Thrice...one even went to court. It is not easy to fight a media house, you see. These people are very well connected...and the owners also don't want public defamation of their company. They put all their money to win or suppress the case."

"Arindam enjoys the indulgence of the owners?"

"Very much."

"But why? Sexual harassment in the workplace is a crime, isn't it?"

"Why should they care? Arindam is giving them business. The TRP ratings are high...The advertisers are spending a lot of money...why do anything to upset him?"

Rinita had no answer, also it was not a question which sought an answer. Going to the police, something she was contemplating, was not an option anymore. Complaining to the higher management was also ruled out. If someone as smart as Chaitali could not survive in RTC without obliging, how could she? On the other hand, the job was too dear for her to let go.

The news that the cafeteria man was getting too friendly with Rinita did not take much time to reach Arindam and he, out of a mixed feeling of envy and suspicion that the old man could jeopardize his intensions, decided to take immediate action. As a part of another perfectly orchestrated plan between Arindam and his partner in crime Souvik, one evening, they along with a few other loyal colleagues visited the cafeteria for some coffee.

Arindam walked up to Mr Gupta, exchanged greetings and enquired about his health and his family – something he had never done in the past, also something he seldom did with anybody he did not have any direct business with. Mr Gupta knew something was fishy. Arindam ordered coffee and croissants for everyone and took a seat with his colleagues.

Mr Gupta balanced the cups on a tray and went up to the table to serve them. As a mark of respect, he decided to offer the first cup to Arindam. Balancing the wide tray on one hand he freed the other to pick up a cup from it. While he was serving the first cup with the hot cup gripped between the thumb and the index finger of his right hand and the tray delicately balanced on the left, he felt a push from behind. The tray tilted and the cups fell down. Hot coffee dropped on Arindam's shirt. Arindam sprang up from his seat and shouted in what appeared a spontaneous reaction, "What the hell are you doing?"

"Actually I...I was...like..." stammered the old man out of nervousness.

"Look at what you have done; you fool...if you can't do your job, why don't you sit at home?"

Mr Gupta tried to explain, but his attempts drowned in the fierce high volume drama played out by Arindam and company.

After a fair bit of acting, Arindam ordered Mr Gupta, "Meet me in my room tomorrow morning."

He then left with his team without bothering to make any payment.

◆

Next day, Rinita found a young man behind the counter. She asked the young man about Mr Gupta but he did not seem to have much of a clue. He could only say that he was temporarily brought in on a very short notice. Now why the vendor company had to bring in a new person was a question Mahesh was able to answer. Arindam had got the old man suspended for six months. Suspension for him meant sitting out of work and losing half his pay.

Rinita could suspect the real reason of the suspension and because it was her, she felt it was her duty to try to do something to help the old man. But how could she do anything without facing Arindam? After all that he had done to her, how should she face him asking for a favour? If she gave him another opportunity, he could interpret it as a compromise message. Or could it be that as he had already achieved his goal he wouldn't treat her specially any longer? And wouldn't asking for a favour from Arindam be like dropping the last bit of self-esteem? But was her self-esteem more important than Mr Gupta's survival? Why should the poor man suffer?

Rinita spent the night debating with herself, but by dawn when the koel sang its morning call, Rinita had reached a decision.

◆

Rinita having overcome the initial hesitation, dashed into Arindam's cubicle.

"May I know why Mr Gupta is suspended?" she asked.

"Please be seated," Arindam said in a cool and composed tone.

"Can you tell me the reason?" she ignored his advice.

"Of course I can…but first you sit and have some water. You look anxious," Arindam pushed a glass of water towards her.

Rinita ignored the water too. "He is a poor man... he has a family of four to support."

"Then he should be careful and attentive at his job."

"See, it might have been an accident…and accidents are accidents, right?"

"May be…but I thought he genuinely needed some rest. He will be back in six months."

"How will he manage in half pay for six months?"

"How am I to know that? Should it be my concern?" The initial kindness in Arindam's voice seemed to be receding. He peeped into his laptop, brushing the mouse pad with his finger. The indication was clear – that he had more important work to attend to.

Rinita was desperate to not let the poor man suffer because of her. She had to negotiate a deal.

"Is there any possibility that his suspension can be withdrawn?"

"If you say so." Arindam spread out his hands in a way to suggest whatever Rinita wished could be done. The eye contact was back.

"I am saying so," she said firmly.

"Then be it," said Arindam, his hands spread out wider. Arindam enjoyed the uncharacteristic display of generosity.

Rinita took a few moments to realize that the job was done: it had been a breeze.

"Thank you so much Arindam da," Rinita's expression had gratitude written all over. But just when she was about to take her leave, Arindam's voice could be heard again. "What are you doing this evening? I have two tickets for King Lear...."

Rinita looked into Arindam's eyes. Arindam was already looking into hers. She could see a wicked smile; she knew she had to pay a price.

"Nothing," she said.

◆

As agreed, at half past five in the evening, while Rinita was patting her lips with a tissue to remove the excesses of freshly applied purple lipstick, her phone rang, indicating Arindam's arrival at her doorstep. She locked the door behind and took the stairs to the ground. To her surprise, she found Arindam standing next to a dazzling Black Mercedes C Class.

Arindam's face lit up at the sight of a gorgeous looking Rinita in a purple salwar suit, matching accessories and a pleasantly surprised expression walking cautiously, placing gentle steps towards him.

"The Chairman's car," Arindam submitted. "I had a meeting with him at his office this afternoon and borrowed the car for the day…he is flying out of the country for a week."

Rinita got the answer to her curiosity without having to ask a question.

Arindam displayed some chivalry in holding open the car door inviting Rinita in. The chauffer knew exactly where to go.

The initial discomfort between Rinita and Arindam kept circling inside the closed cabin of the C Class, with neither of the two speaking, and each looking out of the windows on their side. Rinita looked around inside the car for something interesting and without much effort found a glossy magazine peeping out of the seat pouch on her side. She pulled it out and turned the pages. The business magazine offered nothing matching up to her taste, except the branded products advertised. Rinita's eyes got stuck at the back cover where a black-and-white Aishwarya Rai flaunted a Longines watch – the tagline read 'elegance is an attitude'. Rinita flipped the magazine again and again, and on each occasion, spent more time on the rear cover.

The Shakespeare play was kind of over-the-top for Rinita, who was happy to find both Lear and Cordelia die in less than two hours, drawing the curtains down and Arindam not doing anything to discomfort her.

Arindam dropped Rinita home in the C Class, and contrary to Rinita's fear, didn't offer anything – dinner, tea, coffee or ice-cream.

Rinita entered her flat, shut the door behind and went up to the window from where the Mercedes could be seen being driven away. She took a deep breath. The evening had passed eventless, but Rinita knew there were more evenings to come and all evenings wouldn't be like the one she had just had.

◆

One week later, while she was removing make-up after her bulletin, Rinita received a message that Arindam had asked her to meet him in his cubicle.

"This weekend our team will be going to Digha to cover the inauguration of the Digha Beach Festival. I want you to be a part of this team."

Rinita was surprised at the proposition of an independent outdoor assignment. There were other anchors who were more senior, more experienced and more deserving than her, she thought. Why should he give me the opportunity?

"Outdoor is real journalism...don't let the opportunity go. I offer opportunities to all by turns...this is your turn." Arindam read Rinita's mind and offered a convincing reasoning.

"But will I be able to do it?"

"Of course. There is always a first time for everybody. I also had a first time." Arindam made sure Rinita's confidence was boosted.

"And Souvik and the others will be there to help you...just in case you needed any."

"Well...I..." Rinita groped with her words.

"Don't have to take a decision right away. You can tell me by tomorrow morning. I will have to arrange for someone else otherwise. Anindita or Payel..."

"I will do it," Rinita confirmed promptly without giving Arindam a chance to call out more names. She could not lose to Anindita or Payel, both senior anchors and equally unkind towards her.

Arindam smiled inside; his medicine had worked.

The waves retreated wetting Rinita's naked feet, as if the sea god had issued orders not to breach the 'laksman-rekha' by moistening her beyond that level. The cold water, the orange aura of the setting sun, the speedy breeze had a refreshing effect on her. Rinita needed a break but couldn't afford leave in the first year of job, and therefore the Digha Beach Festival came as a welcome relief.

The inauguration was scheduled for Sunday morning, when the chief minister would fly-in on his way to the Maoist hit extents of West Midnapore. The RTC crew invaded Digha on Friday evening, much before the other channels did, to make sure they got their cameras put up at the best locations, creating the right angles and bagging the celebrity interviews.

Digha looked much different from what it normally did – with everything lit up in bright lights, water-sports, music and art exhibitions, branded food stalls and more.

Rinita had a lighter work schedule planned for Saturday, which presented a perfect opportunity to get away into the fir forest on the left of the Sea Coast Hotel in which the team was put up.

On Saturday, therefore, she rushed through a few celebrity bites in the morning, finished off the brunch she had ordered to her room, and headed towards the fir trees.

The soft sand bed, the tranquility of the trees, and the cool breeze offered a perfect setting for a disturbed mind to revert to peace. Rinita sat at the foot of a tall fir facing the sea, listening to the roar of the waves. The water brought back memories of Phoolbari village, Hooghly river, the abandoned temple and her childhood days with Chaitali and Mahesh.

"Will you marry me Rinita? I love you so much." Mahesh stood before her dressed like a groom in a thick bordered dhoti and embroidered kurta holding a 'topor' – the traditional wedding headgear in his hand. Rinita dressed as a bride in a red Benarasi sari and heavy ornaments laughed heartily at the proposal, and squeezing his cheeks assured, "Of course I will."

Rinita's mobile rang aloud, putting an abrupt end to the dream she had been seeing in her nap. She took some time to get back to reality and answer the call. Souvik was looking for her for some emergency work meeting at the Sea Coast.

"Room 302...fast," said Souvik before hanging up.

"We are the only media house to have managed an exclusive interview of the chief minister tomorrow. Also, I will have the privilege to fly with the chief minister in his chopper to Midnapore and cover the visit first hand."

Rinita could hear Arindam from outside room 302.

"Oh Rinita, where have you been? We had to start without you. It's a prestigious occasion for us...we need to make it a success." Arindam paused his speech to welcome her.

"He will be flying in the CM's chopper...completely unplanned visit," whispered Souvik, dropping in from somewhere, making some effort to supplement Arindam's claim that his visit wasn't planned.

"Whatever," she shrugged her shoulders as if she did not care though in her mind she knew it wasn't a happy situation for her any longer.

She did not pay much attention to what Arindam or the others discussed during the rest of the meeting.

Arindam threw a team dinner at the restaurant where the team ate, drank, puked; some got intoxicated and the others got busy controlling them.

Rinita returned to her room, changed into her nightwear, switched off the lights and went to bed. She could still hear her revelling colleagues. After almost half an hour, there was a knock on the door. Rinita wrapped a stole across her shoulders, switched on the light and answered the door. A heavily drunk Arindam stood there, resting both his hands on the door frame on either side.

"May I come in?" he slurred rather politely.

Rinita hesitated, looking at which Arindam explained. "Actually I do not have a room booked. All the rooms in this hotel and other hotels are completely sold out, and all my colleagues are sharing rooms. You are only one staying alone."

"Does it mean it becomes my duty to share my room with you?" Rinita asked, clearly refusing to buy the argument.

"Not duty lady...favour. If you please."

"Come in." Rinita knew she had little choice; to shut the door on Arindam's face would certainly drop curtains to her career at RTC.

"Thank you so much," Arindam murmured while stepping inside the room. He shut the door behind. Rinita stood back and watched while he walked with unsteady steps up to her. He took out something from his pocket and held it out to her. "For you," he said. Rinita reluctantly un-wrapped the box to find a Longines Dolcevita.

Arindam noticed the sparkle in Rinita's eyes. "You won't forgive me, isn't it?" he asked in a soft voice. Rinita stood still without a word, with her head pointed downwards at the Swiss marvel.

"I am sorry...will you forgive me?" he said bringing his lips closer to hers as he held up her face.

Rinita had, on the one hand a precious tangible object – something she wished she owned but couldn't afford; and on the other hand, a beggar of sexual favours (though not admitting to be one at that moment). She knew she had no escape from Arindam if she had to pursue her profession in Kolkata; given his power, clout and contacts, he could jeopardize chances of her pursuing anything within his sphere of influence. Rinita stood with her back against the wall; she could either refuse Arindam and risk all that she had worked for and dreamt of, or surrender to his designs and negotiate all the goodies she craved for. If she had to lose her dignity, why lose it to a violator for nothing; rather trade it for worldly gains, she reasoned to herself. It wasn't an easy conflict to address; her self-esteem was put up for trade. Self-esteem, the one thing even the poorest of the poor would have. But what value would there be of a hollow self-esteem if its price was so high that all other things of desire would remain elusive forever. And even if some honour could be salvaged, what about that which had already been lost? It could never be recovered, no matter what path she would consciously choose.

Rinita shut her eyes and let Arindam kiss her, the Dolcevita tightly grasped between her fingers.

Over the next few months, nothing remained hidden in the immediate circle of Arindam and Rinita – whirlwind romance was what people at RTC would call the relationship in public, however in private everybody knew Arindam's capability of wooing girls he desired through charm or coercion, or both. The old timers had seen similar steamy romances with Anindita and Payel. All the pretty girls in their prime enjoyed the privilege of sharing the bed with Arindam, living a five star life and occupying a position of power and privilege at RTC, until some other pretty face snatched his attention away. Those who dared to counter Arindam's advances had to quit the organization or profession or town.

Rinita, like Anindita and Payel, walked the path of what some would call a compromise and others a carefully constructed deal.

Arindam did little to hide from his colleagues his particular affection for Rinita. It was not even possible, as all the important shows, critical lives, celebrity interviews and lucrative outdoors started to be assigned to Rinita, defying all protocol of seniority, experience and efficiency. Rinita initially followed a denial policy, especially because she did not want Mahesh to get a clue of what was happening lest he should get upset, but as she could feel the benefits of the relationship showing up in the respectful conduct of seniors and peers, she became more assertive. Also, she felt a compulsive urge to flash all the newly acquired pricey belongings to a larger audience, especially those who had fallen out of favour.

Arindam repeated the style he had perfected over years, of keeping his muse in good humour through a liberal shower of expensive gifts, be it designer clothes, accessories, modern gadgets, and a premier quality lifestyle in the best of clubs, hotels, parties, premiers and events. Rinita clubbed with the biggest stars in Tollywood (some faded stars of Bollywood as well), partied with the richest industrialists in town and dined with the most powerful politicians in the state. In return she did what she would have done every night for an average earning middle class husband at home. Rinita was living a dream.

Arindam was a perfectly charming, well mannered, chivalrous gentleman to all who had surrendered to his wishes. Through his behaviour never let Rinita feel that she was merely playing a whore in his life and that her work was only to quench his sexual fantasies. Rinita, being rather inexperienced in the game, fell for what she should have not. Her feelings for Arindam grew stronger and stronger, until one day three months later she felt dizzy and had a blackout while in office and was counselled by all to seek medical advice.

◆

Rinita was standing by the window of her bedroom. The window spread wide open and the pleasant dusk breeze blew into her face. From the window she could see a park where some children were playing, sliding and swinging. She was blankly looking out holding the grill with both hands, the doctor's question bouncing in her head – "When did you have your last periods?" he asked after doing some blood and urine tests.

Rinita felt an ache in her head, the nerves on her brow felt like they would tear apart. She went up to the cupboard and pulled out a Disprin from the medicine box and turned towards the jug for some water. She paused, thought something and put the Disprin back to where it belonged. She tried Arindam's number for the seventh time since her return from the clinic almost an hour ago; it was still busy.

Arindam called back after five minutes. "What happened? Is everything fine?" he asked.

"I need to talk to you…it's urgent."

"Yes, but today I am in Siliguri. You know that, right?"

"Yes I know. When will you be back?"

"We can talk now."

"No, I need to talk in person."

"Tomorrow afternoon. Let's meet in the evening. I will text you the place and time later. By the way, everything is fine, right?"

"Let's talk tomorrow." Rinita hung up.

The bar at Princeton Club was where they met at eight in the evening. Princeton had been preferred over Bowler's because Rinita wanted a quieter place.

"What is the matter dear?" asked Arindam doing something with his mobile. Rinita waited for some time for Arindam to pay more attention. But when he got no reply to his question, Arindam asked again, this time looking up.

"Yes dear?" he asked.

"You are not listening," was Rinita's reply.

"Of course I am." Arindam got back to touching the screen again.

"I am pregnant."

"What?" Arindam looked up in surprise. He placed the phone on the table, looked around to check whether he had any acquaintances at the nearby tables, brought himself closer to Rinita and asked, "How?"

"What do you mean 'how?'" Rinita could not control her anger.

"Okay, okay...calm down," Arindam cajoled.

"What do we do now?" asked Rinita in a panic-struck voice.

"How many weeks?"

"Six."

"Good." Arindam blew a sigh of relief.

"What good?"

"An abortion should not be a problem."

"How mean! I am not thinking of an abortion."

"Not thinking means what? You want to raise my illegitimate child?" Now it was Arindam's turn to get more anxious.

"Why illegitimate? We can get married."

"What nonsense! I am already married."

Rinita kept silent in the hope that some other better idea would come to Arindam's mind.

"Why didn't you take the pills I asked you to? " continued Arindam.

"Please do something Arindam. I don't want to kill the child." Rinita's voice trembled, her eyes got moist.

"Abortion is not killing; the baby is not born yet." Arindam made a desperate attempt at convincing Rinita.

"I want to keep the child Arindam...as a memoir of our love."

"Love? What love?" Arindam reacted violently this time. "We as consenting adults have agreed to have sex. There was no love."

Rinita had tears rolling down her cheeks.

"Remember, abortion is the only solution. And don't you dare to tell this to anybody." Arindam thumped the table and walked out of the bar, leaving Rinita alone.

For some time Rinita remained astounded at the sudden outburst from the usually chivalrous Arindam. Curious glances descended on her from nearby tables. The waiter in charge rushed down to upright the flower vase on the table.

"Are you alright madam?" he asked Rinita who started feeling nauseous. Before another word could be uttered, Rinita rushed to the ladies washroom and threw up. Rinita felt dizzy and sat down on the floor. She had no strength to lift herself. How to get back home was a much bigger question.

After some time, she heard a loud banging on the door, and a female voice asking, "Madam, are you all right?"

The door was not locked from inside. She only had to twist the handle which she did without having to leave the floor. Two lady security attendants helped her to the security room.

Rinita was made to sit on a chair beside a table fan.

"Can you get my mobile please? I have to make a phone call. It is inside my handbag."

The lady rushed to fetch Rinita's belongings and returned in no time. Rinita took out the mobile and spent some time to decide whom to contact. She dialed the first name which came to her mind, but before Mahesh could pick up the phone, she disconnected it.

After a short pause, she dialled Souvik's number.

◆

"Mahesh is repeatedly calling," Souvik turned to Rinita, looking at her blinking phone.

"Disconnect it. I called him before calling you."

Souvik thought for a second and accepted the call.

"Hi, this is Souvik. Actually Rinita called you by mistake...we are on an assignment...everything is fine...see you in office...bye."

Souvik ended the conversation.

Souvik silently drove towards Rinita's place. He was wise, rather courteous not to ask a single question about what had happened.

Rinita placed her head on the head-rest, the window glass rolled down to let the breeze in, and also to be ready in case she felt nauseous again.

"You don't want to know anything? How I am here in this condition?" asked Rinita, her eyes shut.

"No...you were in a fix and asked for my help. That's enough for me."

Rinita faked a smile and said, "On the one hand you are his pimp and on the other, you are a helpful gentleman."

"Don't worry...you will have enough time to judge."

Souvik helped Rinita up the stairs to her apartment but refused to go in. "You rest...we will have enough opportunities for formalities in the future," he said while leaving.

❧

For the next two days, Rinita was so unwell she had to call in sick. Arindam called several times, but Rinita did not feel like answering the phone. All her dreams and expectations that a childless Arindam would be overboard with joy to know a blood child was coming were already shattered. However, she wanted the child – to feel her tiny little fingers, to hold her, and to feed her with all the milk she would have in her. Rinita did not know it was a girl or a boy, but because she always wanted to have a daughter, she visualized a little girl child. In a way, she was thankful to Arindam for this beautiful thing, and also in a way thanked herself for having missed a few pills. She no longer cared whether Arindam would or wouldn't accept the child as his. All she wanted was to give birth to the child and raise her with the best she could afford.

The bell rang and Rinita answered the door to find Mahesh anxious about her health. They spent a good evening together, rewinding into the past until it was time for him to leave. Rinita went up to the door to see him off. Mahesh had stepped out, but turned back and in a serious tone said, "Take good care of yourself, for yourself and others too."

Rinita pondered over Mahesh's last words again and again. Did he understand anything? Or had guessed may be? How much did he know about her intimacy with Arindam?

Few hours later, there was another guest at the door. This time Arindam, in a highly drunken state.

"You won't let me in?"

"Come in." Rinita made her reluctance evident.

Arindam tried to get to the sofa in the living room, but stumbled. Rinita helped him.

"I am very sorry for that evening," Arindam said even before he could barely sit on the sofa, as if that was his only agenda for the visit.

Rinita remained silent.

"I should not have reacted so fiercely. Missing the pills must have been a mistake. The problem is harder for you than it is for me."

"But I don't have a problem." Rinita's reply was firm and poised.

Arindam got slightly shaken by the reply. He thought Rinita would insist he should marry her or otherwise legitimize the relationship. She, he thought, wouldn't let go of the prospect of extorting a lot of money from him in exchange of giving up the claim and the baby. Arindam had heard of similar situations from like minded friends, but had never faced one himself. All his earlier partners were smarter than Rinita – they preferred condoms over pills; they never trusted Arindam or themselves in matters of sexually transmitted diseases.

Arindam stared blankly at Rinita's face, and Rinita continued arranging the spread out sheets of the day's newspaper into a fold to be put away.

"Why should it be a problem for me? I am the mother…I knew fully well whom I was sleeping with and what the consequences of missing a pill could be," she continued realizing her unpredictable reaction had upset Arindam's script.

"Yes, I thought, because you are childless in your marriage, may be you will want to have the child, but now that I know you do not wish to do that, I am free to decide on my own."

Arindam got more and more confused and curious about what could be on Rinita's mind. He could not hold himself any longer.

"What do you want to do?" he asked.

"I don't know. But I love children and I believe that children are god's gift to parents."

Arindam could read the signals rather clearly. He had to dissuade Rinita from any such decision.

"You are a young lady...you have a lot of years to live, to achieve, to enjoy. A child at this stage will harm your life and career. Do you know how difficult it is to raise a child as a single parent? Just think, you could become a star..."

"So you admit I will have to raise the child as a single parent?" Rinita cut him short. "It is my life, my child. Let me decide," she concluded.

Arindam got furious at the last words. "It is my child too. I will have an equal say," he screamed.

"Don't shout. This is not your office." Rinita's reply was equally loud.

"Listen, whether you are the father is yet to be proved. But that I am the mother is evident, because the baby is inside me...Now you can lift your ass and get lost."

Arindam had never seen Rinita like this before; anger, frustration and desperation if mixed in right quantities would explode exactly the way Rinita did that evening.

Arindam knew it was not his own territory, and any fallout could spell danger for him. He lifted himself and went to the door. Turning back, waving his right index finger, he rolled out the last weapon he had in store. "You will repent for this," he said in a fearsome tone, his eyes rounded and jaw bones hardened.

Rinita didn't return to office after that day. An application for leave of absence arrived instead. The application was supported by a medical note of an obstetrician who had advised three months of bed rest due to some undisclosed gynecological complication. Rinita knew Arindam, and that under his influence, the HR Department would not allow any form of maternity or pre-maternity leave citing some or the other organization policy clause. Thus Souvik, who knew the ins and outs of RTC policies and loopholes, thought of the leave of absence option.

Rinita, during her time of crisis had found an unexpected friend in Souvik. It was a revelation for her that someone, who till the day before was licking his boss's backside had become Rinita's most trusted friend. Was it a form of expression of remorse for his past misdeed or was it part of some plan hatched by Arindam? Rinita did not know the answer; she only knew she had to make full use of whatever support she was getting from anybody. If he would trick her for Arindam's benefit, Rinita would accept it as fate. In any case, she didn't have a better option.

Arindam tried his best to influence the HR Department to reject the application, but in vain. 'If it is rejected, she could go to court... and that would not fetch good publicity for the company,' they argued.

While on LOA, Rinita virtually disappeared. Arindam employed all his efforts to find her, even appointing a detective agency. He cajoled, bribed and threatened Souvik to reveal anything he knew about Rinita, but ended up with nothing. Souvik managed to trick him into believing that he was the last person Rinita would trust. "Why should she trust me, Arindam? Doesn't she know the shit she is in today is because of me too?"

Arindam had seen conviction in Rinita's eyes. He was sure she would definitely give birth to the child. It petrified Arindam to imagine his illegitimate child would live and grow and someday return with a vengeance to destroy his reputation, and claim a share of his property. To prevent all that from actually happening, he had to act, and act fast.

The agency did everything from quizzing her friends in Kolkata and Phoolbari, the doctor who had signed her medical certificate, her neighbours in her Kolkata flat and her ex-colleagues at Shekhar's beauty parlour, but with absolutely no success.

◆

Rinita spent the afternoons in the wide verandah of Souvik's old and sprawling home in Barasat in the outskirts of Kolkata, drying pickles in the sun with his mother. Souvik was the only child and his mother was the only other living family member. The house was big and secluded. Rinita, being a known face on television, was strictly advised not to venture into the verandah without hiding a good portion of her face. Souvik took her out in his car only on the days of her medical check-ups. The only people allowed to visit the first floor of the house were the maid who would sweep and wash the floors, and Mahesh.

Three months passed and the initial dangers of a risky first pregnancy were gone. The baby was growing and growing well inside her womb. Rinita had heard the heart beat during an ultrasonography. Her world revolved around the unborn child. The fact that she was all alone in this big bad world since her mother's death did not hold true any longer. She did not think about her career or worried about the future.

Rinita re-joined office with yet another medical certificate requesting the organization to allot her lighter and shorter shifts at non extreme hours – that is not very early or very late in the day.

Pregnancy was one medical condition which could not stay hidden for long. In her case too, it became more and more evident from the way she carried out her physical activities. Rinita could guess the gossip doing the rounds, but she remained indifferent and unperturbed. This was the world she would have to live with for the rest of her life. Life wouldn't be easy either for her or her child, she knew. She had taken a decision; looking back was not an option anymore.

Rinita and Arindam bumped into each other in the news room on the seventh day after her resuming office. Many curious eyes followed the encounter, which ended, to their disappointment, in exchange of greetings and enquiry of health.

The same evening, Rinita, who had an early evening bulletin was instructed to continue because the evening anchor had called in sick at the last moment. Rinita continued the evening bulletin and at around ten, the late night anchor took over. The exhaustion showed on her body; she had a bad waist pain. Souvik had been sent on a special evening assignment. Mahesh along with most of the others had left for the day. Not many people, except for those who had night shifts, were expected to be around at that hour.

Rinita removed her make-up and picked up her purse, ready to make a move. Arindam waited outside the make-up room until she came out.

"Hi, can we talk for some time? I will drop you home...if you do not object," Arindam said.

"Thanks, I will manage. And let's talk tomorrow." Rinita walked on.

Arindam walked along with her. "Come on, you can spare five minutes for a cup of coffee, can't you?" he said from behind.

Rinita kept walking.

"Please. I said I am sorry. I deserve another chance." Arindam was desperate to have a talk.

Rinita paused, thought something and said, "Okay, where? Five minutes only."

"Let's go to the cafeteria. Will take the lift...I know stairs are difficult for you at this time." He grinned as if he was doing her a great favour.

At the cafeteria, Arindam got two cups of coffee from the automated vending machine and handed one to Rinita. The cafeteria was empty.

Rinita sipped the coffee and asked, "What?"

"Please be seated." Arindam dragged a chair.

"I am fine standing."

Arindam pushed the chair back.

"What?" Rinita asked again.

"How is the baby doing?"

"Good." Rinita was curt.

"The baby is not yet feeling the necessity of a father?"

"Not at all...and never will."

Arindam's face changed. "Why are you doing this?" he said in a raised voice.

Rinita could smell danger, she started retracting her steps towards the lift and the stairs. "Doing what?" she asked.

"You want to blackmail me, right? How much money do you need? Tell me, you bitch...."

Rinita could not control herself any longer, the word bitch hammered on her head.

"Ah, there you are...in your true colours!" she replied.

Arindam fumed with anger.

"I should have known you are incapable of anything better," she continued.

Arindam grabbed Rinita by the spread of her hair and pushed her against the wall. Rinita lost her balance at the sudden violent action and banged her head against the wall. As an instant reaction, she held her stomach in a desperate attempt to protect her child. Arindam dragged her by her hair and pushed her on the floor, shouting swear words all along. "You bitch, you bastard, you whore!"

Rinita hit the floor, her hands still on her stomach.

"I will teach you the lesson of your life!"

Arindam kicked her stomach with his heavy boots – once, twice and thrice. Rinita folded her legs, taking them close to the stomach. It hurt like hell. She cried out in agony; her face contorted in pain.

But Arindam was not done yet. He pushed her with his leg, dragging her to the edge of the staircase. Rinita clutched his feet but could not hold on.

"Go to hell, you bitch!"

Arindam gave the final push with his foot and forced it out of Rinita's clutches. Rinita rolled down the stairs and landed at the first landing five steps below. She groaned in pain, but there was no one around to hear her.

Arindam brushed his hair with both his hands, composed his look and took the elevator down.

Fortunately Rinita was wearing a long skirt with a pocket, in which she had kept her mobile. She could barely take out her mobile and dial Souvik's number. Souvik picked up the phone from the after premier party, and amidst the loud music, the only word he could hear was 'cafeteria' before Rinita fainted. Souvik sensed that something terrible had happened, and rushed back to office, heading straight for the cafeteria.

Rinita regained consciousness after three days of swaying between life and death. She opened her eyes with great difficulty and looked around with blurry vision. She could see the nurse gently brushing her brow. Souvik, Mahesh and Mr Gupta were standing around the foot of the bed.

Rinita looked around and asked the nurse, "How is the baby?"

"Thank god, you have survived. The injury was so serious..." replied the nurse.

"How is the baby?" Rinita's voice faded out of an unexpected fear.

"We have lost the baby," said the nurse, without showing any emotion or sympathy.

Tears poured down Rinita's eyes, her lips flickered. She moved her face away from the nurse and looked down the bed. Mr Gupta started crying aloud, Souvik had silent tears in his eyes and Mahesh wore a serious look, but no tears.

The nurse left the room. Rinita cried for some time until it was time for the police to do routine enquiry. "I went there for some coffee and while taking the stairs down, I slipped," she told the police.

"How did your stomach hurt so badly?" asked the officer.

"I fell on my stomach. It hit the edge of the stairs."

Souvik and Mahesh returned to the room after the officer left.

"Why didn't you tell them the truth?" Souvik asked.

"The baby is gone. How does anything else matter?" was all she could say.

◆

Many would have expected Rinita to never return to RTC. Proving them wrong, Rinita resumed office after a month long recuperation.

As a dear friend and well-wisher, both Souvik and Mr Gupta advised her not to go back to RTC. Mahesh had no opinion on the matter. But Rinita was firm that she wouldn't run away from facing the reality.

"I fail to understand why you want to be back in that hell... won't you find a job elsewhere?" asked Souvik.

"I will tell you when the time comes," came the reply.

Gossips did the rounds again, and people behaved more strangely than what they normally did. Most of the workforce at RTC had known by then the entire story end-to-end. And Arindam, though surprised to find Rinita back, presented an indifferent look, as if he never had anything to do with whatever had been happening in Rinita's life.

One month passed by and the dust settled. No longer curious eyes stared at Rinita; no new gossip could be heard. On one such afternoon, while Arindam was in his cubicle busy with some paperwork, a message beeped on his mobile: '*Miss u*' was the message; the sender, Rinita.

Arindam thought it was a prank by someone who had got unauthorized access to Rinita's mobile. But again, next day, he received another message from Rinita's number; this time it read '*I miss ur big thing. Let's get over the past.*'

Arindam could not ignore the message, but wanted to take cautious steps. He thought he should make some eye contact with Rinita first. Acting on his thought, he deliberately started coming across Rinita's way in office, every time trying to establish eye contact. On the third occasion, the crossing of paths happened at a rather secluded place, and this time, Rinita looked at Arindam too. Eye contact was established and Arindam believed he had seen a faint smile on her lips for him.

She is a real bitch, he thought, having forgotten everything so easily and so fast. She said she missed the big thing; Arindam missed her warm cunt too. Who else would settle for pills, allowing him to enter the depth of her pathway without the rubber shit? The thought of the warmth of her juices wetting his rock re-ignited his craving for her. He rushed to the washroom, entered a commode cabin and dropped his pants. The big thing was up. He held it in his hands and shook hard until it oozed out white liquid.

Their eyes met a couple of times more, and meeting of eyes elevated into exchange of smiles. One day, on which Rinita had a late night shift, she texed Arindam: *'Dying to be f***ed. Make-up room at 10'*.

Arindam checked through the duty roaster of every department in the night shift and made some last minute changes to ensure only old timers were on duty, those who had seen Arindam spend a lot of time with young ladies behind the locked make-up room.

Exactly at ten in the night, Arindam entered the make-up room. Rinita was removing her make-up. There was a repeat show scheduled to run till twelve, thus the make-up room was no longer required for the night. Rinita turned to him and looked deeply into his eyes. She was wearing a light blue bra which Arindam had gifted her, and a long skirt. Arindam's rock was already on the rise.

"At last," sighed Rinita coming close to Arindam and brushed her lips against his.

"Let's celebrate the reunion with some whisky...see, I have your favourite scotch," Rinita whispered into Arindam's ears.

Arindam could not believe it was really happening.

Rinita took out a bottle of Teachers from a cupboard, and poured it into two flat-bottomed glasses. She poured some cold soda into it. She looked well prepared for the escapade.

She offered a glass to Arindam, who overcoming his initial surprise at the dreamlike reality, spent no time in gulping the contents.

Rinita went to the switch board and put off all the lights. Only the bluish dim emergency light illuminated them. The romantic setting was complete. Rinita dropped her skirt. She stood in her lingerie and ankle high leather boots. She brushed her hand over Arindam's pants. She slowly undressed Arindam, dropping one piece at a time – first the shirt, then the vest, then the pants and finally the brief. She made him another drink and sat down on his knees, gently caressing the rock with her fingers.

Arindam gulped the second peg too, and held Rinita by her shoulders and pulled her up to make her stand in front of him. He felt his head was swinging. "I am feeling dizzy," he said.

Rinita was waiting for this moment. She pushed Arindam against the wall and kicked his erected rock with her leather boot's wooden sole. Arindam held his thing and groaned in pain. Rinita showed no mercy and kicked him again, this time on the testicles. Arindam fell on the floor, rolling in pain, holding his penis. Rinita put on her dress and switched the lights on. She lit a few matchsticks and held it up close to the smoke alarm; the alarm rang. Rinita opened the door and squeezed and twisted Arindam's penis and testicles against his body and the floor with her heavy boots while waiting for a crowd to gather.

The alarm led the crowd to the make-up room, where, to the astonishment of all, they saw Arindam lying on the floor, fully naked, holding his private parts, groaning in pain and Rinita pressing on his external genitals with her heels. The crowd gathered, but none came to Arindam's rescue. Some clicked snaps on their mobiles; the others looked on with suppressed laughter.

After enough people had witnessed Arindam's drubbing, Rinita pulled out a piece of paper from her handbag, threw it on Arindam's face and walked off.

"So this is why you wanted the drug," asked Souvik turning on the ignition. His face glowed in contentment.

Rinita smiled.

"What was the paper about?" he asked while driving out of the RTC car park.

"Resignation letter."

The car disappeared speedily into the darkness of the night.

PART 2:
Priyanshu Agarwal and Hemant Thapa

By the time Rinita collected her luggage and stepped into the arrival lounge of the Bagdogra airport, it was late afternoon. A short, thin and fair man held out an A-4 size printed paper which had 'Rinita Bose, Wellington Tea Estate' written on it in bold letters. Rinita faced no difficulty in locating Chetri, the driver at Wellington who had come to receive her.

Rinita, in her sports shoes, jeans, tight top, oversized shades covering a good portion of her face and silky black hair tied in a ponytail bouncing behind her shoulders looked no less than a movie star. Since Chetri had no clue what Rinita looked like, he made all attempts to ensure every lady travelling alone got a glimpse at the paper he held out.

In an attempt to grab the attention of the other ladies, Chetri missed out the one who mattered. Rinita walked up to Chetri and waved her hands in front of his eyes which were roving in a different direction. Chetri turned to Rinita.

"Hi, Rinita Bose. I think you are looking for me," Rinita introduced herself.

Chetri looked at the paper he held in his hand to confirm the name; he never expected his guest to be so glamorous.

"Gautam Chetri, madam."

Rinita acknowledged the delayed reciprocation by offering her hand. Chetri brushed his right palm on his pants to ensure it was clean enough.

◆

The blue hard top Maruti Gypsy picked up speed on the Hill Cart Road, running through the dense Mahananda Wildlife Sanctuary which had only the toy train rails running in parallel.

"You couldn't see me coming?" asked Rinita seated next to Chetri.

"Actually I thought you were some movie star," Chetri replied shyly.

Rinita burst out into laughter at Chetri's reply, more at the way he had said it, rather than what he had said. She laughed heartily for a couple of minutes. A tiny teardrop trickled down the corner of her eye, reminding her that she was laughing her heart out after a long time.

"What made you think so?" Rinita asked Chetri, not because she wanted to know the answer, but because she wanted to enjoy another shy expression from Chetri.

"Actually there are many beautiful shooting spots around this area...and many people from Kolkata come to shoot here."

"That's fine, but what made you think I was one of them?" Rinita wouldn't stop unless she got to see the shy expression once again.

"You looked so smart and beautiful." Chetri gifted her the expression she was looking for.

Rinita laughed out again.

"How far is the garden?" Rinita, having laughed enough, tried to change the subject of discussion.

"Ghoom is sixty-six kilometres from Bagdogra, another fifteen kilometres downhill is the garden."

"Must be beautiful, right?"

"Very beautiful madam, you will love it...there is also a Kanchenjunga view point."

"You can see Kanchenjunga from inside the garden?"

"Yes madam."

"That's fantastic." Rinita almost jumped up in excitement.

"You can see Darjeeling town right in front. It is just across the valley."

Rinita could wait no more to get to the Wellington Tea Estate where she had joined as a Junior Labour Relations Officer. While the Gypsy climbed the spirals of the mountains, Rinita retraced everything that had happened over the past twenty-two days, starting with walking out of RTC and ending with an offer letter for a job about which she had no prior experience or knowledge.

"What do you have in the other bag? You have not unpacked it," asked Arundhuti while combing her hair in front of the mirror.

"Things which I do not need frequently."

"Don't hesitate to use this room like your own. Stay as long as you want or need...and make yourself absolutely comfortable." Arundhuti smiled at Rinita.

"I am absolutely comfortable dear," Rinita's response acknowledged Arundhuti's kind gesture.

"So, what are the less frequently used things?"

"Some party wear costumes, books, etc."

"Oh ho...then you better unpack them, dear. We might have a grand party coming up this weekend."

Arundhuti headed for her shoot, leaving behind her small but reasonably organized room at the working ladies hostel at Rinita's disposal.

Rinita had been staying with her friend and one time colleague during her modeling days Arundhuti since the RTC episode.

She shifted out of her rented apartment moving all her belongings to Arundhuti's place, among which was the king-size VIP bag which Arundhuti was talking about. It was impossible for Rinita to maintain her expensive accommodation, also it wasn't safe any longer, given the fact that Arindam had been there many times. Though Souvik had repeatedly assured Rinita that Arindam was wise enough not to pursue the matter any further, legally or otherwise, as it would expose all the misdeeds he had inflicted upon her, Rinita could not be assured.

Four days had passed since she had shifted to Arundhuti's place and she had not ventured out. Some unknown fear that Arindam being wounded as he was would be out for revenge, had set upon her. But staying indoors was not a long term viable option for her as she had to start searching for a job.

Rinita looked at the strolly bag and feeling slightly refreshed about a possible party decided to unpack it. She pulled out a few party dresses. She thought she was done and was about to bang the lid and set the number lock into a random combination when she noticed the corner of a book peeping out from under some garments. Rinita pulled out the book – *Gandhi Meets Primetime: Globalization and Nationalism in Indian Television* by Shanti Kumar – gifted by Arindam on Rinita's birthday in an attempt to enlighten her about her job. Rinita flipped through the pages of the book which she had never read.

Rinita found a book mark inside and turned to the page where it took her. The object rather than the position it represented caught her attention. It was industrialist Prem Agarwal's business card which he had presented to Rinita during the shoot of a commercial of his product, Wellington Tea, in which Rinita had played the lead model.

Rinita pulled out the card, shut the book and placed it back. The book was of no significance to her any longer, but the card was. She brushed the card on her cheek, trying to recall more details of the meeting.

Dark clouds rushed in from the other side of the river. The clouds brought in gushing wind, uprooting the setting put up by the set designer on the lawn of the Radisson Fort Hotel, the venue for the shoot for the Wellington Tea advertisement, the first major break in Rinita's modelling career. The assistants and technicians ran across from one place to another, arranging for covers for the expensive camera and lighting equipments. Rinita, in her pale yellow sari, a costume carefully designed to match the theme colour of a Wellington Tea pack, stood out in the verandah of the room she was using as her make-up room, enjoying nature's tryst.

There was a knock at the door. "Come in," said Rinita without looking back, assuming room service might have come to deliver the tea she had ordered.

"Ah, there you are!" A sweet middle-aged female voice announced to Rinita.

Rinita turned back to find Manju Parekh, the Corporate Communications General Manager at Wellington Tea, the lady who had chosen Rinita for the role, standing behind her. Behind Manju was a tall and fair man in a brown suit.

"Meet Mr Agarwal, the Vice Chairman of Wellington Tea Private Limited," Manju said pointing at the man in the brown suit.

Mr Agarwal was old, most likely in his sixties, but lean and stout. He was bald with thin grey-brown hair along the periphery, but that he had been handsome at his prime could be anybody's guess.

"Hello. Nice to meet you," Mr Agarwal said in a deep voice.

"Nice to meet you too, sir." Rinita was quick to respond.

"Mr Agarwal has come over to see the shoot," said Manju. "But it seems we may have to cancel it...anyway Mr Agarwal has a small gift for you."

Manju handed over to Rinita a large box of Wellington Tea. It was the first time Rinita had actually looked at the product she was out to promote.

"Thank you so much. But will the shoot get postponed?" Rinita's expression of anxiety was well read by Manju.

"Do not worry, whenever it will be shot, it will be shot with you," she assured her.

Manju's phone rang and she took her leave. "We will have to get going. I will talk to the director and keep you posted."

Manju left with Mr Agarwal. Rinita went back to nature.

◆

The shoot was planned for two days. Day one got washed away in sudden torrential rain. But day two, thanks to the nature gods, from the very morning saw sparkling sunlight from above some scattered white and grey clouds. Everything around looked fresh and clean and bright, as if god had cleansed the earth and the venue to ensure that best quality pictures and videos could be shot.

Directions from Manju were rather clear: two days' schedules had to be completed in one, so that the budget wasn't exceeded, and the entire cast and crew got down to achieving it. By the end of the day, while dusk was falling, Manju lifted her eyes from the monitor, where she scanned through the entire day's hard work and pronounced, "Excellent!"

The technicians, who till then had held their nerves, jubilated and congratulated each other on the success. The director was found smiling. Nothing else apart from the client's acceptance mattered to him.

Manju congratulated the team, shook hands with all, and promised a party to celebrate the success of the campaign, where Mr Agarwal would personally thank the team. On her way out, she noticed Rinita, the prime attraction of the pictures and video shot throughout the day, standing near the door with her back against the wall. She flashed a thumbs-up signal and said, "Stunning." Rinita smiled back in acknowledgement.

◆

Gift coupons, instead of cheques, came as gifts from Mr Agarwal in the party held in the evening the advertisement was released on television. The party at the ballroom of Oberoi Grand in Kolkata had a giant screen put up which had visuals coming from a popular Bengali entertainment channel, in which during the first break of the mega soap which started at 8.00 p.m., the Wellington Tea commercial was supposed to be telecast.

The break came up at ten past eight when Manju made an appeal to the audience to observe silence and focus on the screen. And then, after a Bollywood superstar had demonstrated some heroics post consuming a cola based drink, Rinita, in the pale yellow sari, appeared preparing, having and blissfully enjoying the aroma and taste of Wellington Tea. Stunning Rinita would certainly lure a lot of people, especially men, to drop a pack or two of Wellington Tea into their shopping bags.

The crowd clapped and cheered, and Mr Agarwal handed over the gift coupons of ten thousand rupees to each team member. Rinita, the director and the chief cinematographer got bigger value coupons, worth twenty-five thousand of a Kolkata-based leading jewellery store.

During dinner, Mr Agarwal, along with Manju, went up to each guest, congratulating them on the occasion and playing the perfect host, encouraging them to enjoy the food and drinks. When they came up to Rinita, Manju said, "Ah, here she is who needs no introduction. Mr Agarwal is extremely pleased with the way the commercial has shaped up, isn't it sir?"

"It is fantastic...and you are fabulous," he said looking into Rinita's eyes. His expressionless face, and eyes, which she felt could penetrate deep inside her, made Rinita uncomfortable. But Agarwal was a man who meant business and business alone. He took a business card out of his coat pocket and offered it to Rinita. "I am very impressed with your work. Keep my card. You can contact me if ever I could be of any help to you."

"Keep mine too," Manju popped out her card.

Rinita politely accepted both and put them inside her purse.

Over the past few days, Rinita had thought of a couple of possibilities: getting back to modelling or rejoining Shekhar's. Joining a rival news channel or agency was not an option as Arindam enjoyed a lot of clout within the media fraternity. Also, Rinita didn't feel safe living in Kolkata. The best option would be to find employment in some other city, but Rinita didn't have the education or experience to bag a decent job in any other industry.

Rinita dialled Prem Agarwal's number, but before the phone rang, disconnected it. Calling Manju was a better option, she thought, and went to look for her card.

Rinita dialled Manju's number; Manju was more than happy to give her an appointment.

"Tell me dear. What brings you here?" asked Manju while making tea for both of them inside her beautifully furnished room in the Wellington Tea Private Limited office in Park Street.

"I have not been seeing you on television these days," she continued before Rinita could answer her first question.

"Actually...I am no longer with RTC."

"Oh I see." Manju offered the tea and looked at Rinita rather curiously.

"Frankly, the situation became so complicated that I had to quit."

There was a long pause, with Rinita hesitating to divulge any details, and Manju waiting for Rinita to do the talking.

Realizing that Rinita might not be feeling comfortable opening up, Manju asked her, "I guess you are here because you need some help."

"I am looking for a job outside Kolkata, may be in some other city…far away."

"Any particular reason?"

A pause again and this time Manju decided that she'd have to drive the discussion, and to do that, the ice needed to be broken.

"You want to have some pani-puri?"

Rinita, busy framing in her mind where to start her story, got rather surprised at the strange offer, but before she could respond, Manju already rose from her chair.

Rinita, like any other Bengali girl, was very fond of puchka, what Manju called pani-puri. Manju wanted to take Rinita out in the open, and she would have done it anyway.

Manju drove Rinita to Outram Ghat along the banks of the Hooghly river.

"Inhale some fresh air and tell me why you have left a lucrative job at RTC and want to leave the city?"

Rinita remained silent.

"Dear, if you do not tell me everything, I will not be able to help you."

◆

"Hmm. Allow me to feel sorry for you. You are a strong woman to have withstood such emotional and physical pain, and fought back. Hats off to you dear."

Rinita felt strained every time she re-lived the cruel times at RTC, but Manju's words comforted her. She had her eyes fixed on the setting sun on the western banks of the Hooghly river, the side of the river where Phoolbari village was situated few kilometres upstream. Often Rinita would remember the innocent childhood days at Phoolbari, and how her life had changed over a distance of just fifty kilometres.

Manju noticed no change in Rinita's expression; her wound must have started to bleed, she thought.

"Let us take a walk," she said.

"So, what kind of job are you looking for?" Manju continued with the conversation.

"Anything."

"Your skills in modelling and media will be of no use if you are looking for a job in an industry like ours."

"I know. I deliberately want to stay out of the media."

"Hmm, let me talk to Mr Agarwal. I will be happy if we can do something for you."

"Thank you."

"I will set up a meeting with Mr Agarwal. Let's see what happens. By the way, do you know Wellington Tea's market share has grown by twenty-five percent since the commercial you did for us?"

Rinita shook her head suggesting she didn't.

"You are lucky for us...tell me where can I drop you?"

◆

"Come, come!" Manju peeped out of Mr Agarwal's room and called her inside. Rinita stepped inside the big room with wooden walls and expensive paintings – the room of the Vice Chairman and Managing Director.

"Please come in, Miss Bose. Please be seated," Mr Agarwal said warmly. Rinita sat on the chair opposite to him. Manju occupied the chair next to hers.

"Mrs Parekh just told me how our market share increased after the commercial. We knew it would do well, but twenty-five is phenomenal. A good amount of credit should go to you, Miss Bose."

Rinita was impressed with the sophistication with which Mr Agarwal conducted himself. She smiled at the compliment.

"I will come straight to the point. I have a flight to catch in less than two hours," he said taking a look at his watch. "We have a vacant position of a Junior Labour Officer in our garden. If you wish, we can place you there. It fulfils both criteria: it is far away from Kolkata – fifteen kilometers from Ghoom in Darjeeling hills, and it does not have anything to do with the media."

Agarwal looked at Rinita, who came up with a mixed expression of excitement and anxiety.

"You do not have to say 'yes' or 'no' straight away. Mrs Parekh will explain to you what Wellington Tea would expect from a Junior Labour Officer. We will close this when I am back after three days."

Rinita did not have a reason to disagree.

Rinita and Manju took Agarwal's leave and stepped out of his room.

"A Junior Labour Officer's job must be a difficult job, right?" Rinita asked as it was a serious sounding job profile.

"I will not be able to help you, but I can take you to somebody who can – Joydeep Sarkar, former Senior Labour Officer, now Vice President Human Resources to whom you will be reporting."

"He sits in this office?"

"Very much, travels occasionally to the garden."

They walked down to the other side of the office and Manju knocked on a door.

"Come in please." A smart heavy male voice invited them in.

Manju and Rinita entered the elegantly decorated room, though smaller than Mr Agarwal's.

"Let me introduce your new junior, *Miss* Rinita Bose." Manju made sure Rinita was clearly visible to Joydeep from where he was seated. "She is joining as the Junior Labour Officer to be posted at the garden," she continued.

Rinita found strange that Manju should emphasize so much on the 'miss'. How did it matter, she wondered.

"Rather attractive as well...please be seated." Joydeep took away his eyes after a brief glance at Rinita.

"She is slightly worried about the role, so I thought I should introduce her to you. You can explain to her what her job will be all about," Manju said to Joydeep while both of them looked directly into each other's eyes. They seemed to be communicating more through the exchange of glances than through words.

"Hmm, Mr Agarwal's new recruit?" Joydeep asked. His tone suggested he wasn't too optimistic about the quality of work Rinita would do.

"So, you two get on with your discussion. I will have to take your leave now," Manju looked relieved to have handed over Rinita to Joydeep.

"Please be seated, Miss Bose." Joydeep was too polite to disclose his thoughts to Rinita who was thrust upon Joydeep as his junior by Mr Agarwal without any consultation.

"Tell me Miss Bose, what do you want to know?" Joydeep rested both his hands on the table and joined them through fingers crossing into each other. Rinita appreciated the posture – it was accommodating, encouraging and polite.

"Do you...." Rinita had just started speaking when Joydeep cut her short.

"Do you appear on television?" he asked.

Rinita nodded her head in the affirmative.

"Must be the news...because that is the only thing I watch."

"Yes."

"That's why you look so familiar."

"I did a commercial for Wellington Tea as well."

"Oh yes, I remember watching that too...tell me where can we start?" Joydeep's bringing up of the television topic relaxed Rinita's nerves.

"I do not have any training or experience for the job I am being asked to do."

Joydeep shrugged his shoulders and said, "I was also not trained or experienced when I took up my first job as a labour officer. I was a lawyer, but with no particular fascination for labour laws."

Rinita employed the maximum amount of attention she possibly could afford.

"The purpose of what I just told you is not to indicate that a lawyer's qualification is well suited for this role, but that training and experience is not a very essential criteria," he continued.

"What you will be required to do is to maintain a fantastic relationship with the labour union men, understand and appreciate their problems and grievances, report them to the head office – more precisely to me. But remember, never assure them of any solution. Only the top management or board, not even me, is entitled to decide what and how much to give away. If you face any problems, pick up the phone and talk to me."

Joydeep paused for a little while and continued.

"The bottom-line: it is not something you will not be able to manage. On the contrary, a charming lady like you is perfectly suited to help keep tempers under control at the site of labour activity."

Joydeep's words made the job seem easier than what it really was, and Rinita started believing there wasn't a reason why she shouldn't be able to manage it.

"But I want you to hang on before you take the final decision on whether or not to accept the offer. Just wait." Joydeep picked up the phone, dialled an extension and said, "I am done explaining to Miss Bose the role and responsibilities. Can you please drop in?"

Minutes later, Manju reappeared into the room and reoccupied the seat next to Rinita.

"So what do we do now?" he asked Manju.

Manju had no answer to offer. Rinita wasn't sure what could possibly be left to be discussed.

"I think we should ask Julie to have a chat with her," said Joydeep.

Manju, though reluctantly, made a hand gesture which meant 'let be it'.

Joydeep picked up the phone again and asked somebody to come to his room. A tall, fair, slim, pretty lady in a formal skirt, top and high heels, entered the room.

"Meet Miss Julie White, Mr Agarwal's secretary...and she is Rinita Bose, our new Junior Labour Officer to be posted at the garden. I have explained to her what the organization would expect from her as a Junior Labour Officer. We want you to have a discussion with Miss Bose about any other specific expectation Mr Agarwal would have."

"Come with me for a coffee, Miss Bose," Julie was quick to understand what was expected of her.

"Please," Joydeep asked Rinita to go ahead while Manju looked down.

Julie led Rinita to Mr Agarwal's room and ordered two cups of coffee over the phone. While they waited for the coffee to arrive, Julie cleaned up the files and papers lying on Agarwal's desk.

"Mr Agarwal is a very straight forward person. He is sixty, sober and elegant." Julie sipped at the smoking coffee and said before going for another. She stood in front of the only window in the room and looked outside.

Rinita had nothing to say, so she remained quiet. After a long pause, Julie continued, "Mr Agarwal thinks you are very attractive...and could be a good company."

"Okay." Rinita grew impatient with every pause and wanted her to come out straight about what expectation Mr Agarwal had.

"Sir visits the garden on an average once a quarter; whenever he goes he stays for three days."

"Okay."

"During his visits, he likes to relax, to enjoy his whisky and the natural beauty of the mountains."

"Okay."

"He travels alone, but like any other human being, he enjoys quality company."

Rinita got a feel of what could be coming. She had had enough experience of knowing powerful men.

"Like all men, he likes the company of women – young, attractive."

There was a long pause from Julie. She continued to look out of the window into the sky. She never made any eye contact with Rinita.

"Do you mean he is expecting sexual favours from me?" Rinita thought there was no point beating around the bush any further.

"Sir is no longer a very potent man. He is incapable of establishing any sexual relationship with anybody. At his age and with the medications he takes to fight prostate cancer, he is very safe company for women. He is fond of watching nude women. The feeling of having a desirable woman at his disposal satisfies his ego."

"Hmm..."

Julie had very clearly spelled out expectation lying before her. The reason for Joydeep's asking her to hang on for the time being was now clear.

"So Miss Bose, I have done what I was asked to do. Now you may get back to Joydeep sir and Manju ma'am."

Julie turned and made eye contact with Rinita for the first time ever; clearly the discomfort from her side had slightly abated once the point was made.

Rinita got back to Joydeep's room and took her seat.

"Take your time to think about it, Miss Bose. There is no hurry. But please do not discuss this outside the four of us," said Joydeep.

Rinita shook her head to mean she wouldn't do that. "I'll take some time to think," she said before leaving.

◆

Two days later late, a message reached Manju's mobile, which read, *'It was a difficult decision. He is a sick man...and I have seen worse...Accepting the offer'*.

'Thank you,' texted Manju right away.

"Pull up the window madam, it will get colder from here. We have just crossed Kurseong." Rinita was woken up by Chetri; she did not realize when she had fallen asleep. Through the windscreen she could see the mountains through dense fog and descended clouds. The rich greenery of the fertile Himalayas, the dampness of the air, and the pine trees on the valley side of the road welcomed her to a paradise where she would have a new beginning.

Rinita rolled up her side of the window and while the car turned through a hairpin bend, she pointed down at tea bushes arranged in perfect discipline, like pieces of green sponge glued to the ground all along the walls of the slope they had just crossed. "What garden is that?" she asked Chetri.

"That is Makaibari Tea Estate, world famous for flavoured tea."

Rinita wondered whether Wellington would also be as beautiful as Makaibari, or even better. What a beautiful place to live and work in, she thought.

Rinita had never been to the hills earlier. Her life started and had gone by in the plains of Bengal, up and down a particular stretch of the Hooghly river. She had only heard stories and seen pictures of the beautiful Himalayas. What she felt with her own senses was much beyond what she could conjure from the amateur stills of domestic photography or professional cinematography of masterly crafted movies. The heavenly land had won an ardent admirer.

The distance of twenty-five kilometers to Ghoom from Kurseong flew in forty minutes. Rinita's admiration for nature had by then entered an eternal loop. Chetri slowed his car as he neared a settlement. "There is a beautiful monastery at Ghoom. Would you like to take a break and stretch your legs? Beyond this point, we will not find a village until we reach the garden."

"It is beginning to get dark. Will it be safe to spend time here?"

Chetri smiled at Rinita's concern. "The drivers plying on this route know each bend by heart," he said.

Rinita opened the door and the chilly air hit her. She pulled out a full sleeved sweater, wore it and jumped out of the car. "Will you come with me?" she asked Chetri.

"I have certain things to buy from the shops. We can meet after fifteen minutes," he said making it clear that he had his own agenda.

Rinita took the downhill road to the monastery, the gradient jerked her knees. The brightly coloured construct of Buddhist architecture had a fifteen feet statue of Maitreya Buddha. Rinita lit a lamp, and rolled her hand over the sequentially arranged prayer wheels praying for a blessed start to a new life.

"We will leave the Hill Cart Road here to take the right. Hill Cart Road goes straight to Darjeeling which is less than eight kilometres away. Have you been to Darjeeling?" Chetri asked while turning on the ignition.

"No, but I will this time."

"You should. It's beautiful."

The fifteen kilometres towards the right from Ghoom was a road on which villages were few, gardens and forests plenty. The bluish light of the dusk was good enough for Chetri to see the road, but Rinita's excitement had started showing traces of fear of the unknown. "Don't we have headlamps?" she asked.

"Yes, we do."

"Then why don't we put them on?"

"It will scare the animals." Chetri's last words were reason enough for Rinita to insist on the headlamps. She was in no mood to spare the animals a scare at the altar of herself. Chetri obliged.

Soon, a large white wooden board welcomed them to the Wellington Tea Estate. Chetri drove the Gypsy up a curved gravel driveway, starting adjacent to where the welcome board stood and ending at the foot of a cluster of three bungalows – one big and two small, all equally beautiful.

The manager of the estate, Shekhar Dutta, a grey-haired, middle-aged man of medium height and build, welcomed Rinita. His wife Sunaina – short, plump and very seldom seen without a knitting kit – joined him. They escorted Rinita to the bigger bungalow, the director's bungalow, and unlocked the guest room for her.

"We live in the manager's bungalow, the smaller bungalow on the left," said Sunaina. "The other bungalow is for the Resident Medical Officer and the Chief Accountant. The other officers and staff have quarters slightly higher up near the view point," Shekhar added, pointing to a series of lights arranged at a point higher up in the mountain.

"We were asked to make arrangements for you here," Shekhar's expression while uttering these words meant to say 'we know the reason why such special treatment is being rolled out for you'.

Over the next fifteen minutes, Shekhar and Sunaina bombarded Rinita with a lot of information: some of which missed her attention and some of which she deliberately ducked because they were not immediately relevant. Rinita made sure she had learnt enough about the basics required to spent the night peacefully and comfortably; the rest, she thought, she could assimilate over a period of time.

Shekhar and Sunaina's part as perfect hosts couldn't be complete without a dinner invite which Rinita had to accept, though she would have loved to grab whatever was available and throw her tired soul into the nicely made fluffy bed.

At the nicely laid out dinner at the manager's bungalow, the menu was thoughtfully selected – from fried fish to mustard fish curry; fish which must have been brought over from the plains cooked in typical Bengali style. At the dinner, Rinita learnt that the Duttas had a ten-year-old son who studied in Darjeeling, and that Sunaina recovered from acute melancholy during the initial days of her stay in the mountains secluded from civilization, and some other less important things which she chose not to let register in her mind.

◆

Rinita had an uninterrupted peaceful sleep which broke because of the loud chirping of the birds. She also realised that the thick quilt that looked rather confident of keeping her warm the evening before hadn't been enough. Either there must have been some room heating arrangement which had extinguished or the mornings were disproportionately colder, she thought. A thick streak of golden morning sunlight finding some room between the closely drawn drapes had entered without permission to flood a portion of her bed. Dust particles were dancing along the lighted beam. Rinita lay in bed for some time, watching every bit of what she saw and felt. It was a perfect setting for a vacation where one would have lazed around all day, but Rinita was here for work, she had to report to the manager's office at 10.00 a.m. The same man who had played a lovely host the previous evening would, wearing some formal expression, check her offer acceptance letter and other credentials.

Rinita wrapped a shawl, went up to the window from which the sunlight barged in and drew the drapes apart. Through the window pane blurry with morning dew, she could figure out an expansive tea garden which ran into the valley on one side and climbed the mountain by another thirty metres on the other. The sky was bright with white clouds floating on the blue expanse.

Rinita stepped out of the bungalow in formal wear, with a folder containing all the papers necessary to prove that she was herself and that she had a legitimate job at Wellington to join.

"Ah good morning, Miss Bose. Hope you had a good night's sleep."

Rinita heard Shekhar's voice from her left. Rinita saw Shekhar reading a newspaper while having tea on a garden tea table arrangement laid within ten feet of his bungalow's entrance, something she had not noticed the previous evening in the dark. She went up to the table with a smile.

"Join us for tea," he offered. Noticing that Rinita was more interested in the paper he was reading he said, "Yesterday's paper... want to read? We are always one day behind the rest of the world," he said laughing out loud. Rinita joined the table.

"Did you have breakfast?"

"No."

"Why? Where is Lama, the attendant of your bungalow?"

"I don't know. I have not seen him since morning."

"Oh these people...must have had too much to drink last night. I am so sorry. Make sure he is there to attend to you all the time. Tea, coffee, breakfast, dinner – all that is his responsibility. If he is not doing his duty, tell me."

"I will."

Rinita had her bed-cum-breakfast tea together in one cup of smoking black Wellington Darjeeling. Rinita was not unknown to the taste of Wellington tea, but the making at the Dutta's was certainly different; it pulled out the best of aroma and flavour.

On the breakfast table spread with bread, butter, omelette and boiled vegetables, she gathered some necessary information about what she saw around.

"The garden is facing north-west. The Kanchenjunga is slightly to the west of where Darjeeling is. It can be seen clearly early in the morning. There is a Kanchenjunga view point higher up in the mountain. You can get a spectacular view from there."

Rinita confirmed the directions, as told by Shekhar, with the position of the sun – indeed the sun was shining from behind the mountain, most likely from a north-easterly direction. In summer, that was the normal position for the sun, she knew. She also saw the factory, slightly down the slope towards the left. "The office is adjoined to the factory...Are we good to go?" Shekhar asked.

"Yep," replied Rinita, eager to see her office.

While walking down the road leading to the office, Shekhar showed her where the workers lived and where they shopped for essentials, both places being within the territory of the three hundred and fifty acre garden, one of the largest in the vicinity.

At the office, Rinita found a small but beautiful room waiting to be occupied by her. A big bouquet of colourful orchids specially made to welcome her was presented by her colleagues – some locals and some from the plains. After the initial formalities were over, Rinita sank into the revolving chair and picked up the cradle of the land telephone positioned on her desk and dialled Souvik's number.

"Do not share the number with anyone, not even Mahesh. I do not want Arindam to get a clue of where I am or what I am doing," she said.

"I have never let you down, except for once for which I have repented enough. You can trust me."

"I do, otherwise I wouldn't have called you..."

There was a knock on the door. Shekhar came in with a young man whom he introduced as Hemant Thapa, a plantation supervisor and more importantly, leader of the incumbent labour union.

"As a labour officer you will have to deal the most with Hemant...and he is a difficult customer," Shekhar said as an extended introduction. Hemant was young and lean and had sharp eyes, but the fact that he didn't smile while shaking hands with Rinita worried her. Hemant was a typical union leader, she though, who wouldn't exchange pleasantries with the management, especially the labour officer who was supposedly his number one enemy. At the end of their icy introductory meeting, neither of them took away any positive impression about the other.

Before lunch, Shekhar dropped in with the production manager and together they went to visit the factory. The production manager explained to Rinita the processes and essentials of tea manufacturing. As they walked from one floor to another, he explained pointing at each work area and machinery the technology used in drying, grading, cleaning and packaging. Rinita lent her best attention as an obedient student. Never had she imagine that such massive post-plantation activities were involved before the tea hit the cups.

Over the next seven days, Rinita read a lot of files, documents, paper cuttings and legal notices, some of which she understood on her own, some with the help of Shekhar and others, some not at all. But the enthusiasm and perseverance she exhibited impressed all thosc who had seen the initial expression on her face when the files had been heapcd onto her table, and the contrasting interim expression of contentment and confidence after seven days of intense reading, which included her first weekend spent entirely inside her room with the reading light on.

She read about the history of the garden – about how the ownership fell from the British to the Agarwals, changing hands twice in between, the productivity graphs, and how it linked with the rain gods and labour unrest, the export figures, and the economic challenges from low cost fake Darjeeling products, the terms agreed between the management and the union when the garden reopened after a prolonged strike over wage, and contract labour regularization demands.

In between her busy schedule, she managed to find some time to see the first rains pouring from the black clouds which appeared out of nowhere one evening. She also rose early one morning and with minimal help from Lama climbed the Kanchenjunga view point top to watch the golden first rays of the sun hit the pointed crowning, and captured the heavenly moment with the six megapixel fixed lens camera she always carried. On her way back to the bungalow for lunch, she paid careful attention to the perfected technique exhibited by the ladies in nipping off the apical portion of the shoots.

It was her eighth day in the garden, the day she had confirmed to herself that she had read through all the files made available to her and had understood a good amount of them, she left office slightly earlier than usual to enjoy the falling dusk in the open. She took a *pagdandi* going down into the valley to have a closer feel of being inside a tea forest. The pagdandi progressed in a serpentine line, sometimes straight into the valley, sometimes towards the left or right, getting steeper at times and falling flat at the other. After climbing down almost half a kilometre, Rinita could hear a babble of streaming water coming from the valley. Feeling excited on having discovered, without any assistance, a water body she had not been told about, she speedily rushed down a few more steps until she could see a moderately thin stream of water, descending from a hilly waterfall. Rinita selected a convenient position under a shade tree for a photograph. She pulled out the camera from the backpack and held the viewfinder before her eyes. But what she saw through it ran a cold shiver down her spine. A thin black snake with faint yellow horizontal stripes, not more than three metres in length hung out of the shade tree under which Rinita stood, with barely two feet distance between itself and her, looking straight into her face. Before Rinita could react to the unpredicted catastrophe, she heard a male voice calling out, "Don't move!"

Rinita abided, though she wasn't sure whether the instruction was intended for her; definitely not for the snake, she was sure. After almost one whole minute of patient glance exchanges between Rinita and the serpent, Hemant Thapa emerged from her right with a stick, a broken branch rather, and poked the snake with it. The animal twisted itself around it. Hemant carefully withdrew the stick and along with the snake, threw it far into the valley.

"Cobra," he said looking back at his enemy number one at the garden, the Junior Labour Officer Rinita Bose. "Not often found at these heights," he continued. Rinita stood shivering out of fear.

"Relax madam. It's gone...nothing to fear anymore."

Rinita fainted, but before her body could drop on the ground, Hemant held her by her waist.

The faint light of day-break crept into the room in which Rinita murmured in a feeble voice, her first words since the previous evening. Lama, uncomfortably positioned on a chair, entrusted with the responsibility of attending to Rinita in all her needs, woke from his nap. His instincts told him, and past experience of nursing the sick, that water was the first and only valuable thing a patient would require, if he or she was waking up after a long time. He poured some water into Rinita's mouth, which seemingly satisfied her enough to put her back into sleep.

Later in the day, Rinita woke up more convincingly. It was then that Lama informed everyone concerned and soon Rinita's room saw many guests: Shekhar, Sunaina, Hemant and an unidentified middle-aged gentleman who carried basic medical equipments. He tested Rinita's chest with the stethoscope, counted her pulse, pulled the skin at the bottom of her eye to check the blood levels and declared her fit.

"What happened to me?" asked Rinita, oblivious about the happenings between the previous evening and then.

"You saw a snake in the garden and fainted," said Hemant.

Rinita took some time to get hold of her immediate memory. "Yes I remember...cobra...not found often at this height, you said...but why did I faint?"

"It is because of the trauma...nothing to worry, you are absolutely fine now," said the doctor.

"But you need to get some rest. Mr Dutta, let us leave her alone," he continued while rising from the chair on which he was perched.

"Absolutely," affirmed Shekhar and soon the room became empty, only Lama waited for Rinita's instructions – whether he was to stay or leave.

"You also go and rest." Rinita was sure she needed no more help.

Left alone, Rinita fixed her eyes on the ceiling, and could not help but remember the intensity with which the cobra had looked at her. She felt a shiver and goose bumps, but realizing that she was far from danger, she adjusted the blanket to cover herself better.

◆

After one complete day of rest, Rinita re-joined office, and the first thing she did was to call Hemant to her room. She respectfully offered him a seat and served him tea she herself had made. Hemant had not felt so important within the garden premises ever before.

"Will you take me to the stream again?" A weird request from Rinita started the conversation.

"Of course, why not?" replied Hemant, though he was not sure whether that was the only thing she wanted from him.

"When can we go?"

"We can start around half past four so that we can be back before dark."

"Done. Meet me outside this building."

Hemant waited for some time, but realized that was all.

Hemant turned to open the door when she said, "Don't forget to carry a stick."

Hemant smiled and left.

◆

"So, how long have you been here?" Rinita asked Hemant while climbing down the slope.

"My entire life," was the expressionless reply.

"How many years would that be?"

"You mean my age... twenty-seven. My parents worked in this garden."

"They don't any longer?"

"My mother passed away and my father retired...he was a security guard."

"Sorry to hear about your mother."

"You will be more sorry to know how she died – starvation."

Rinita paused, lifted her eyes to look at Hemant. The expression on her face suggested a mix of surprise and shock.

"Before the Agarwals took over, the garden was shut for a number of years. No work in the garden meant no earnings for the people. Whatever little savings we had, she spent on feeding us: me, my father, and my sister, while starving herself."

"How old is your sister?" Rinita asked, wanting to change the course of the conversation.

"She would have been twenty-five had she been alive."

"My god...and how?"

"Started with a stomach ache, which we later came to know was appendicitis. The appendix burst."

"Oh my god...she must have suffered."

"She did...she was a brave girl." Hemant's voice trembled.

"But how could it burst like that? There must have been symptoms."

"That time the garden was shut, there were no medical facilities. Even now we do not have a full time resident medical officer. There is a health centre, but in a very bad shape. We keep on shouting, but the management does not pay attention."

Hemant paused a little and continued, "The doctor who attended you was called from a nearby garden."

"That means if an ordinary labourer falls sick, he will not have access to a doctor?"

"Not within the garden. He will have to go to Ghoom town... and for better treatment to Darjeeling."

"That's bad."

Hemant smiled and pointed at the flow of water some six feet away from where they stood. "There you are," he said.

Rinita moved up to the stream and bowed to touch the water; it was cold and clear.

"Where is it coming from?" she asked looking in the direction of the approaching water though the stream hidden behind the bushes beyond a few metres.

"There is a waterfall nearby which is the source. You cannot see it from here."

Rinita sat on one of the larger rocks along the banks of the stream dipping her feet into the cold water. She folded her cargo trouser up to her knee, exposing her perfectly carved calf muscles covered with soft, smooth fair skin.

Hemant standing behind her more like a body guard with the stick in his hand could not resist the temptation to take a look at the portion of skin which was on offer.

"Mr Thapa, you seem more educated than what one would ordinarily expect, aren't you?"

"You can call me Hemant, madam," Hemant replied without taking his eyes off Rinita's exposed feet. "I have done agricultural engineering from Uttar Banga Krishi Viswavidyalaya," he said with such indifference as if it didn't mean much.

"You could have got a better job elsewhere."

"I could have, but I did not want it. I studied agriculture because I wanted to learn about plantations and tea. I cannot leave the garden. This place is everything for me."

Rinita turned to look into the eyes of the man whose conviction impressed her. She noticed Hemant take his eyes off her legs in natural response.

"You are a gifted man, Mr Thapa."

"Hemant," he corrected.

"Friends?" Rinita offered her hand.

Hemant hesitantly touched her fingers. "My honour, madam."

◆

Hemant's humble outlook towards life, simple needs and the conviction of not to excel alone but to make an effort for collective betterment somewhat fascinated Rinita. How could a person, she thought, who had seen so much difficulties in his lifetime shun away from a better job, better pay for his own self to return to stand by and strive for marginal betterment of many more people? There were many people like Hemant, though miniscule in comparison to those whose world started and ended with themselves and their immediate family.

Rinita had known someone like Souvik, whose character suffered from very precariously poised contradictions – on the one hand he had a job to save, for which he wasn't hesitant to act as a confidant to a corrupt boss; and on the other hand, he had befriended and shared the distress of the victim, went out of the way to stand by her in her struggle for justice. At the end of the day, how should Rinita judge Souvik? Was he an ordinarily pure soul whose conscience had momentarily betrayed? Or was he normally shamelessly corrupt unless some extraordinary catastrophe like the one which happened with Rinita awakened the habitually dormant purer part of his conscience. Rinita didn't have an answer, but she remained thankful to Souvik for the extraordinary cooperation he had extended when Rinita had needed the most.

Rinita knew Hemant neither well nor long enough to know whether he too, like Souvik, suffered similar contradictions; but from what she had seen or known till the time she had advanced her hand was enough to initiate friendship.

The brewing friendship between Hemant and Rinita didn't amuse a lot of people at Wellington, especially at the management level. It became such a grave matter of concern that the news reached Joydeep in Kolkata, who, reacting differently from some others blew out the extra air held inside his mouth when Shekhar Dutta delivered the news to him over the telephone.

"I hope you have better things to do, Mr Dutta, besides worrying about friendship matters," he said.

"Oh yes, I do," replied Shekhar, swallowing some saliva, realizing it had not gone down too well with Joydeep.

"Don't worry. I will talk to her. However, the company HR policy does not expressedly prohibit such things."

"I fully understand," was the humble submission from Shekhar before Joydeep hung up.

Joydeep did call Rinita to discuss the matter. In his usual dignified manner, he asked Rinita to be careful not to divulge any classified information outside the management group.

"What made you think I would do that?" asked Rinita, correctly guessing the backdrop of the story.

Joydeep laughed over the phone at her sharp reaction, realizing he had done a very silly thing. "Nothing...absolutely nothing...do not worry," he said making up for his folly.

"I know, sir, why some concerns are being raised, but be assured."

"I am...I am." Joydeep forced a quick exit from the embarrassing conversation.

But back in Wellington, efforts were on to dissuade Rinita from having close ties with the working class.

"I hope you know he is married," said Sunaina one Sunday morning while pouring tea into Rinita's cup. Mr Dutta had gone to Darjeeling to check on his son at his boarding school and therefore Sunaina and Rinita were the only two at breakfast that morning.

"What is that supposed to mean?" Rinita's question sounded aggressive.

"No...actually..."

"Of course. I know his wife was a nurse in a Siliguri nursing home before marriage, where he was admitted for a few days when he suffered from a minor accident. That's where they met and fell in love and eventually married," said Rinita interrupting Sunaina who went groping for words to appease Rinita's anger.

"Oh yes...that's lovely...you know so much...it is always good to know about people..." Sunaina went on blabbering in a desperate attempt to cover up.

It was normal to gossip, thought Rinita, for people who had long passed their youth, when they saw a young man and a young woman spend more time together than what they would want to see. It was pointless to get angry at them, especially when the mindset wasn't a thing which could be changed easily. Rinita laughed inside, wondering how stupid these people were to think that they could be romantically involved, though she remembered in a flash how Hemant had taken his eyes off her naked legs dipped in water; men will be men, she thought and laughed again.

◆

The more time Rinita spent with Hemant, the more she learnt about the grim realities of the garden. The realities at Wellington, she learnt, were no different from what prevailed across gardens – in different degrees depending upon the size, scale and depth of the pockets of the promoters. A multinational company would offer better facilities to the workers as long as the unit was running in profit. But with increased competition from newer sources within and outside India, and a poorly-protected Darjeeling branding, the profit levels were closer to or lower then break even than ever. Once a garden was shut, the workers would die of starvation and malnutrition just like what Hemant's parents and their contemporaries at Wellington had faced.

But that is when the garden was not operational. But even at Wellington, a company operating at full capacity and as per Hemant, making more profits than what gets reported in the books of account, the labour welfare index made a dismal reading. The non-operational health centre building was in ruins, not to mention the complete absence of any medical and paramedical staff and supply of essential medicines. That there was no medical officer at the garden was already known to Rinita who had had a first-hand experience. The school which was set up for educating the children at the garden received no maintenance, had no teachers, and had shamelessly lost its affiliation with the council. The wage levels barely matched the minimum statutorily enforceable figures published by the government in the national gazette.

"Why do you think the tea companies fancy exploiting its people, if I am allowed to use that term?" Rinita asked Hemant while walking alongside through the narrow pagdandi laid between the tea bushes, heading towards his house for a cozy lunch with his family on a Saturday.

"As a management representative, you are not allowed to use that term," Hemant said. Rinita couldn't figure out whether it was sarcasm at display or a thoughtful warning.

"But as a union leader I am free to make liberal use of that word. Yes, there is exploitation, very naked exploitation, especially when there is 'suspension of work' notice pasted on the walls, mainly because no other industry in this region could employ these people. Firstly, because there is none, and secondly, because the 'tea' skill is not required in any other industry. Thus, when the supply is guaranteed, abundant exploitation becomes evident. However, despite this situation, the multinationals, who are generally rather careful about their public image, offer the best working conditions."

Hemant's comprehensive reply rattled Rinita's brains for some time. Unlike trigonometry, which bounced back on almost every occasion, the socio-economic situations of the tea industry made inroads, though slowly, into her mind. The more she assimilated, the more she felt the responsibility as a Junior Labour Officer as well as a human being to contribute favourably towards the betterment of the workers at Wellington.

"But," she said rather hesitantly, not knowing in what spirit Hemant will take it, "the market has also shrunk, hasn't it? I was reading through one of the committee recommendation papers which said Indian's exports share had declined from 20.86% in

1986 to 12.34% in 2008...not sure whether I am quoting the figures correctly."

"Wow, perfect job with the figures, but not much with the inference. The market hasn't shrunk out of nothing. It is India which has lost its market share to other low cost suppliers," replied Hemant.

"And that is a major concern for all concerned, including us," he said more as an afterthought.

That day Rinita had a memorable lunch for more reasons than one. Hemant's pretty wife Mini not only cooked and served exotic local dishes, but also shared with Rinita the kind of elementary medical services she provided to the sick living in the garden, the cost of which was mostly borne out of Hemant's paltry income.

"You never told me that," complained Rinita looking at Hemant.

"She had nursed Sunaina madam when she had broken a leg some years back," proclaimed a proud husband.

Hemant's three-year-old daughter hopped around the room in excitement of having a guest she had not seen or known earlier. When Rinita asked her name, she stopped hopping and hid behind her father.

"Tell your name to aunty." Mini's serious instruction made her pronounce her name, "Varsha Thapa."

"Does she go to school?" Rinita's question was directed to her parents.

"Not yet...we teach her at home along with others," replied Mini.

"Others?"

"Yes, all garden children up to age six, after which they go to the government school seven kilometres away."

"My god...seven kilometres?" exclaimed Rinita. "Why don't we get the factory school going?" she asked.

"That is for you to answer, madam," said Hemant.

"I know...I will try," she assured them.

The little child brought back memories of her miscarriage. She vowed to do something about the school so that the little child wouldn't need to walk fourteen kilometres daily.

That night, while alone in bed, Rinita couldn't resist shedding a drop in remembrance of her lost unborn child.

◆

Over the next one week, Rinita made valiant attempts to get some concession from Joydeep for reinstituting the school, but all she could secure were some building materials which could be diverted from the ongoing renovation at the factory shed. Chalk, duster, blackboard and other basic stationery materials could be paid out of the employee welfare budget, though they needed to be booked in the financials as miscellaneous petty expenses. Joydeep made it categorical in unambiguous language that no official document should record the real purpose of the expenditure.

Rinita could not figure out the reason for such vigil on a matter, which to her, appeared rather non-poisonous for the management, until Hemant explained to her how it could be seen as a precedence of the management submitting to worker's valid rights of education. Truly, there could be so much to read by a seasoned mind into things which appeared rather simple to others on the surface.

She however, went on to make maximum use of the concessions allowed by Joydeep. She got building materials and labour diverted from the factory to the school, got the stationery and text books for the school library purchases done and accounted for just as Joydeep advised. The only key factor which remained to be addressed were instructors, which, they knew, the management would never allow to be hired. Thus, Hemant, Mina and Rinita took turns in teaching the students. Who should teach what was decided based on their mutual confidence and proficiency. Rinita picked up the language and humanities, leaving science and mathematics, trigonometry included, to Hemant and Mini.

It didn't take long for the school to become popular among the garden workers' families who started sending in their children in good numbers. Rinita, Hemant and Mini spent their early summer evenings, lazy weekends, and holidays teaching language, mathematics, science and humanities to the children, who though were enrolled in some distant formal school where they went in only during examinations; the real education happened within the garden. Though the management did not endorse the effort, they didn't play spoilsport either, and the school went on to run successfully.

Two months into their successful venture, one typical monsoon afternoon in the hills, Rinita was teaching ancient Indian history to a group of students. Hemant arrived at the door, extensively drenched, despite being under a full size umbrella. He looked at Rinita, evidently wanting to say something. Rinita walked across the room up to Hemant who whispered something into her ears, after which Rinita did not take long to wrap up the class and make a move towards the bungalow.

Around the director's bungalow, a lot of activities, very unlikely for a Sunday afternoon, could be seen. Two cars – including a Range Rover – were found parked outside the bungalow. Rinita had not seen either of them in the garden before. The manager was found instructing a lot of people to do a lot of things and the house staff looked busier than ever. Other officers who never had any reason to come close to the bungalow were found hovering around.

Prem Agarwal had paid a surprise visit to the garden and had caught them unawares; not even the manager knew he was coming. Rinita made her way through the hustle bustle into the bungalow and got into her room to change out of her wet clothes. After a warm bath, she dressed into a more formal outfit than what she would usually do on a Sunday at home and paid a visit to Mr Agarwal in his room. His room, actually a suite which had a smaller living room and a larger bedroom with attached washrooms in both, always remained under lock and key and was not available for use by anybody else except him or his family.

"Good afternoon, sir," she said.

"Ah Miss Bose, good afternoon."

"Hope you had a good journey."

"It is never good at this time of the year...the chances of landslide and road blockages are higher than ever."

Prem paused at this point and expected Rinita to come up with the next question which could have been 'why then had he taken the trouble to visit the garden at this time of the year', but soon he realized Rinita was new and wouldn't be sure whether it was appropriate to ask such a question to the Managing Director. So he went ahead to explain the reason.

"There was a meeting of the Tea Exporters Association in Siliguri yesterday. Many owners and promoters joined the meeting. Most of us came in the same flight from Kolkata and also had the return booked together, but the flight got cancelled because of the rain. So we decided to get to our respective gardens and spend a couple of days until the weather improves."

"It is our luck to have you here," said Shekhar who suddenly appeared behind Rinita.

Prem smiled at Shekhar's adulation. He knew the flattering types rather well.

◆

For the rest of the day, Prem Agarwal remained busy with wanted-unwanted guests dropping in from the garden, nearby gardens and local authorities, each having their own agenda. By evening, the guest list had thinned down to a handful of Wellington management staff. Prem sent out a message through Shekhar that he would not be available for any meeting after seven. Also he sent a note through the attendant of the director's bungalow to Rinita inviting her to join him for dinner at eight.

Rinita dressed herself in an exotic off shoulder white gown with intricate embroidery on a net base, put nude makeup and left her hair loose bouncing over her shoulders. She had done her homework well, for Prem who had studied and lived a good part of his life in England took fancy in vintage Scotch whisky and fair-skinned westernized ladies.

At eight, Prem was waiting in a formal dinner jacket for the expected tap on his door. But what he saw on the other side of the door was nothing less than a surprise. Prem, who always wanted to out-smart and out-dress his guests, faced a dose of his own medicine. Rinita had bowled him over.

The dinner was arranged in the living room of the director's suite. Necessary arrangements were made to keep the food warm. Evidently, Prem did not want any third party interference, not even the attendants at the private party hosted in honour of Rinita alone.

In an act of impeccable chivalry, Prem welcomed Rinita into his suite. The lights were kept dim, a Beethoven symphony playing in the background and the fireplace was lit up – more for the flickering yellow-orange light than the heat. Though continuous rain had dropped the temperature a good five degrees below normal, it wasn't cold enough to warrant a fire. On a quick scan around the room, Rinita noticed the skylight was tilt open in a way to let the cool breeze come in and get the ventilation going. A gentle intoxicating aroma could be sniffed, but she was not sure where it came from.

Rinita chose white wine over scotch. A tall slender wine glass clattered against a short broad whisky glass and the party began.

Two drinks and Prem offered his hand for a dance. Rinita hesitated as she did not have any training. Prem insisted he could teach the steps better than a professional trainer. And soon, after two circles, Rinita's false footwork toppled her upon Prem's stern frame. Prem loved it – Rinita's gentle intoxication, missing of steps and clutching his arms for support. His eyes sparkled, his muscles tightened and blood inside his veins started rushing in all directions.

More drinks and more dances, and Rinita after another false step dipped her face into Prem's chest. Prem lifted her face by the chin, run his index finger down from the brow to the cheek removing the streaks of hair covering most of her face, and crossed her lips with his. Rinita's eyes drooped from the effect of alcohol. She welcomed Prem's warm lips, her hands made way inside his coat to clutch his chest firmly.

The effect of medication had taken his manhood away, but Prem loved the feeling of possessing the most desirable of women, and no medication could take this feeling of joy away from him. He loved to see women standing naked in front of him, fully surrendered, waiting to be violated. And he, out of mercy, or respect of womanhood, would let them preserve their chastity, without letting out the real reason of his generosity.

But that night was different and Rinita was a different person. Like the other ladies, Rinita stood devoid of even a single piece of string before a fully dressed Prem, with her hair hiding her nipples and her palm strategically perched over her neatly shaved pubic. Prem watched admirably at her near perfect shape, the tone and softness of her skin, and the venerability in her eyes. But soon, the admiration gave way to depression – a feeling of overwhelming loss of not being able to make any use of a golden moment and the opportunity. The pride which he derived by letting the damsels get away after a surrender, he knew, was nothing but a hollow reasoning to hide the larger feeling of loss.

Rinita stood still in the posture for some time. She knew Prem would make no further move and she would eventually get to get away with her honour intact in a few minutes, or maybe longer. Prem continued intensely adoring her desirable body from the sofa on which he had loosened his body, occasionally sipping his whisky.

After five minutes of adoration, Prem was done with his pride. He picked up the pieces of lingerie lying in front of him on the floor and threw them back towards Rinita. Rinita caught them with both hands. But she didn't move, nor did she make any attempt to put on her clothes. For some reason she felt sorry for the man who had lost a good part of his life to a deadly disease. She dropped the lingerie back to where Prem had picked them up from and went up to him. Prem felt a sense of fear of the unknown. He wondered whether Rinita would launch some kind of an attack on him to revenge the humiliation. The effect of alcohol, however, prevented him from any serious defense.

Rinita knelt down before him and untied his belt. She ripped open the chain and pulled down his trousers to the extent possible from that position. Prem did not have the strength to protest or prevent. Rinita pulled down the brief and took the feeble thing in her hand. She caressed it for some time with utter care and then started licking it. The licking of the tip ran a sensation within Prem's body – something he had not felt in years. Rinita sucked it in every possible way but could not make a man out of it. Prem though, despite his limitations of sensation, could derive a feeling which took him fractionally closer to the real thing.

◆

Next morning, though a Monday, Rinita woke up later than usual, possibly because of the effects of alcohol. It was 11.30. She rushed to the washroom and was, ready for office in twenty minutes. On her way out she glanced at the director's suite, only to find it locked from the outside. She asked the attendant about Prem and learnt that he had left for the Bagdogra airport early in the morning. Rinita peeped out at the bright blue sky with scattered clouds hiding the sun and letting it out the next moment. She reached office and found an envelope with her name neatly spelled on it placed on her desk. She tore it from one edge and poured out the contents. There was a small chit which read 'You've earned this for the health center' and a cheque of five lakhs bearing Prem's signature, but without an addressee. Rinita picked up the cheque and reclined on her chair. Can we renovate the building and buy some necessary medicines with that money, she wondered. Also in whose account should the cheque be deposited?

Three months down the line and the hospital building was up on its feet again, with a few beds laid down in the main hall, some basic medicines stacked up in the stores and Mini being the only person to look after it. The paramedical tasks though were taken up equally by Rinita and Hemant, as there was no budget for hiring a full time medical officer or a nurse for the exclusive employment of the hospital. All the three – out of longing to do something beyond their daily routine, something worthwhile – had stretched themselves to the fullest. Perhaps the will to do well brings along with it a lot of power and energy.

A Sunday morning in early October, a lazy day otherwise for all but for the likes of Rinita who would have classes to instruct throughout the day, saw a somewhat deviation from the routine. Rinita was woken up earlier than usual by the sound of the unlocking of a door and some ancillary activities. The first thing which came to her mind was that the director's room was being unlocked; perhaps Mr Agarwal had dropped in for another surprise visit. Peeping out of her door out of some degree of curiosity, she saw that the director's room indeed had been unlocked and some hectic activities were going on inside – dusting, cleaning and sweeping.

She thought she would ask the attendants she encountered what the fuss was about, but instead, while stepping out of her room and turning in the direction of the main entrance leading to the garden, she bumped into a tall and handsome young man carrying a pile of books so high that his vision had been partly obstructed. The books fell and scattered all over the corridor, and the handsome man, so deeply in love with his books, completely ignored the beautiful cause of the accident and got busy gathering them. Rinita joined to help the young man. They didn't get a chance to meet each other in the eye until all the books were gathered and arranged. Rinita lifted her eyes and fixed them on his face, which was still directed at the floor, and said, "I am so very sorry for this."

The young man lifted his chiseled face; his blue eyes met Rinita's. For a moment there was silence, only admiration of a beautiful undone face straight out of bed, a perfectly toned body barely hiding behind a flimsy fashionable nightwear. A strand of her hair flew across her right cheek reaching her lips, the colour of which carried faint traces of the lipstick worn the previous evening.

"It's my fault," he said. 'And I am not sorry,' he wanted to say but did not. Rinita was somewhat lost in the blue of his eyes, but regained herself when he introduced himself. "Priyanshu Agarwal," he said with his hand stretched out, wanting to touch Rinita's on the pretext of a shake.

"Rinita Bose." She obliged with her soft touch.

◆

Priyanshu made rapid progress in finding out more about Rinita, the one person the Wellington management had not shared a word about. Rinita also, though more cautious and discreet in comparison to Priyanshu, did the same about him.

"He is the prince of Wellington, Mr Prem Agarwal's son," said Hemant while locking the classroom door one evening at the end of the last class. He looked up at Rinita's face for a reaction but instead found that she was keen to know more.

"I saw him come to the garden two or three times before, but it never looked like he had any interest in the functioning of the garden. He came, roamed about, enjoyed the climate and beauty and went back. Last time he had come here three years ago, before leaving for the United States to get an MBA degree. Now it seems he has returned and has been asked by his father to join the business."

Hemant said all of this without any pause or break, as if he was on a flatland and not climbing a mountain.

Rinita waited for some minutes to make sure Hemant was done with his initial remarks, and also to catch her breath. Climbing the slope for her was not as easy as for Hemant, though after a few months at the garden, she was doing better.

"He knows you?" she asked.

"Yes, yes…very well. We once had a fight when he in a drunken state stumbled and fell upon the gardener's daughter."

"What? He fell upon the gardener's daughter?"

"Not that he meant to make improper advances. He was too wise to guess the ramifications of being an Agarwal at Wellington."

"Then why did you fight?"

"At that time, I was younger…and the worker-management relationship was strained. He became an easy target for people with vengeance."

"I see…so you people talk to each other?"

"After that incident, during his next visit, the manager asked me to take him for a tour around the garden. I guess it was his father's instructions."

"He went?"

"He did. That is when I realized that he has no interest in the tea business."

"So you two spoke?"

"I had to, because I had to show him things and explain. He did too. He spoke about his US dream, city life and branded living."

"And that is how you concluded that he wasn't interested in tea business?"

"He was not interested in whatever I was showing him."

With this, Rinita and Hemant reached the lawn leading to the director's bungalow. From there, Hemant took the path on the right which went straight to the village, and Rinita went inside the bungalow. None of them noticed Priyanshu who stood in the dark outside the bungalow, having a smoke.

The next day around noon there was a tap on Rinita's cabin door.

"Come in," said Rinita without lifting her head from a file she was carefully reading.

"Hi, I am Priyanshu," said the entrant.

Rinita looked up and responded with a cautious 'hi'.

"I was just looking for company for lunch."

Rinita found the approach rather peculiar, but she appreciated the directness.

"But I already have company."

"I know…Hemant. He is a good friend of mine too. I am sure he wouldn't mind if I drop in."

This fellow has done good homework, thought Rinita. She felt a compelling desire to spend some time with him to understand what he had in his mind.

"Okay, do drop in," she said. She shut the file she was studying and left her chair. "Follow me," she said while walking out of the room.

Priyanshu followed her out into the garden, but before getting down into the pagdandi between the bushes he enquired, "But where are we going?"

"I have lunch in Hemant's house. His wife is a fantastic cook of local dishes. If you want to join us, you will also have to have the same food," she said looking sternly at Priyanshu who looked little unsure at the beginning, but then said, "I love home food."

Rinita knew at once that his love for home food was nothing more than a ploy to spend time with her. But she was happy that she had managed to call the shots.

When they reached Hemant's house, they found Hemant coming from another direction. "Hemant daju, how are you?" Priyanshu said in broken Nepali and jumped forward to hug him.

Both Hemant and Rinita were surprised to witness such exhibition of warmth.

However, Hemant, like a true gentlemen, reciprocated Priyanshu's gesture with whatever was possible in his capacity. The lunch Mini served, though fell slightly short of quantity, did not lack hilly hospitality.

During lunch, they talked about many garden-related things, including the newly set-up school and medical centre. Priyanshu actively participating in the discussion, even congratulated the three of them for the excellent job they had done.

Hemant, who had the impression that Priyanshu was rather snobbish, was surprised at what he saw. Had he mistaken in his judgment or was it that Priyanshu had changed?

After the lunch, Rinita, Hemant and Priyanshu threaded a common path for some time until it was time for Hemant to take another route. "Do you remember once you showed me around the garden and I never listened to what you had to say?" Priyanshu asked.

Hemant smiled but didn't reply. "Will you do that again? This time I will pay a lot of attention, I assure you." Hemant looked at Rinita. The last thing he expected at that hour was such a request. "Of course," he affirmed.

Over the next week, Priyanshu, like an alert pupil learnt a lot of management work from the manager and others at the office, including a few things from Rinita. And about the finer nuances of tea cultivation, he learnt from Hemant. All this time, he made sure he lunched at Hemant's house. He also hosted a dinner for his lunch mates at the director's bungalow one evening. On other evenings, Priyanshu and Rinita had dinner together in the Director's bungalow dining hall, but their conversation would remain rather limited as Priyanshu remained engrossed in some kind of reading material. Not that Priyanshu never tried to strike a meaningful conversation, but whenever he tried to venture into personal territory, Rinita would shut the door. She made it amply clear that she did not appreciate discussing personal matters with somebody she was professionally involved with.

On the last day of Hemant's guided tour of the garden, Priyanshu asked him an out of context question. "What is your opinion about Miss Bose?"

"Regarding?" asked Hemant, failing to draw a link.

"Like...I do not know anything about her personal life...where she comes from...about her parents. You must know all about all these things, right?"

"Certain things yes, but not all. Rinita is rather reserved about her personal matters."

"Does she have a boyfriend?" Priyanshu went straight to the point.

Hemant was slightly surprised at the abruptness and directness of the question. "I don't know. She never mentioned it."

Priyanshu, slightly disappointed, reverted with another one "Do you think I am good enough for her?"

Hemant was not sure what Priyanshu wanted to know. Did he really want to know whether he was good enough for Rinita or was it a trick question which actually meant to ask whether she was good enough for him?

Hemant had to remain non-committal. "Not sure...but why not!"

Just when he thought the difficult conversation had ended, Priyanshu bounced back with another straight one, "Do you think she will say 'yes' if I propose to her?"

Hemant felt like running away from the spot. "I am sorry I do not have any idea.

Priyanshu lost no time in throwing the fourth bouncer at Hemant. "Can you please tell Miss Bose that I am in love with her and would soon ask her hand?"

"No way...it is your job...be a man and do it," said Hemant. It was his most spontaneous reply during the course of the conversation.

◆

Hemant and Priyanshu parted, and Hemant heaved a sigh of relief. But many questions troubled his mind about the recently concluded conversation. Was Priyanshu really in love with Rinita? Was it possible for someone, especially for the flamboyant Priyanshu, to fall in love within ten days of knowing somebody? Could it be that he had some indecent design in mind and he wanted Hemant to be his accomplice? Going by his family history, it was a valid possibility. In either case, Hemant thought, he should have a discussion with Rinita, though it may not be in the line of what Priyanshu had suggested.

Priyanshu had some business in Siliguri for which he was away from the garden for a couple of days. Hemant thought it was a good opportunity to ask Rinita certain things he wasn't comfortable asking with Priyanshu around.

"What does the prince do after work?" he started.

"Are you asking me because I am his next door neighbour?" Rinita asked with a tinge of suspicion.

"Of course, what else?"

"One wouldn't believe that we seldom talk when we are at the bungalow. We meet at dinner where he reads his files and I read the newspaper. Then he goes out for a smoke and does whatever he does in his room. I watch news on television and then doze off."

"Is it? That's rather surprising."

"Not really. Why should a director-in-making talk his heart out to an employee? In my opinion, this is perfect director-ish behaviour."

She didn't reveal that Priyanshu had on a few occasions tried to encroach into her personal territory which she had firmly resisted.

"Director or whatever, he must be a very shy type with ladies, right?"

Rinita looked sternly at Hemant. What is he up to? Did he want to find out whether they were befriending each other? If yes, why? Was he jealous of Priyanshu? Or was it that he wanted them to be closer and therefore, by design, was pushing them towards each other?

Her mind rattled, she couldn't find an answer. But since she had known Hemant rather well, she was confident that he would not do anything which would prove detrimental to her interest.

"Maybe," she replied. "But I won't believe that he never had anything to do with pretty women. He definitely knows how to deal with women. Just that he exercises his discretion."

"Women will understand better," Hemant shrugged. He decided to interview Priyanshu once he was back from town for answers to some questions which had started bothering him. He was pleased to learn, however, that Priyanshu was not causing any disturbance at the bungalow.

It was the third time since she had been in the garden that Rinita had a chance to use her desk phone for personal purposes. The incoming call from Chaitali sounded nothing less than Mozart playing into her ears exclusively for herself. Chaitali and her husband were in India for a holiday and she had taken the pain to collect from Souvik, after a lot of persuasion, her number at the tea garden. Once they came to learn where Rinita was, they decided to squeeze a short Darjeeling trip into their busy itinerary.

"You will be able to make it? You can manage leaves and other things, right?" asked Chaitali.

"Anything to see you dear...If required, I will quit."

The dates were quickly finalized. Within ten minutes of the call, a leave request went out of Rinita's mailbox to her boss with a copy to the manager.

◆

Priyanshu was eager to know whether Hemant had spoken to Rinita, and called up on him the very day he returned from Siliguri.

"Did you get a chance to talk to her?" he asked.

"I told you I wouldn't," Hemant replied.

"Ah!" Priyanshu's expression showed his disappointment.

"Tell me something...aren't you going a bit too fast?"

"What do you mean?"

"You have been here for what, maximum two weeks...and you claim to be head-over-heels in love with Rinita...someone whom you have not known before...and you still hardly know her, as you yourself admitted."

"So what? Time is no measure of love." Priyanshu's dislike for the question was apparent from his tone. Hemant heard the warning bells; he had encroached too far into forbidden territory.

But Priyanshu was surprisingly polite. "I understand where you are coming from, Hemant," he said. "Since I have returned from the US, my mother insists I get married soon. They made me meet a couple of girls within my community.... smart and beautiful, rich and pampered...but I don't know. I don't want to spend the rest of my life with someone like them. I want an independent girl, humble background, self-made, fighting it out every day to make her place in this world...someone of substance, you see."

"Hmm..." Hemant observed without showing any signs of accepting or rejecting the argument. "And you have never met anyone like Rinita before?" he asked.

"I have known a lot of ladies, but all within closed groups. I never had the opportunity to venture out of my class, amongst real people."

Hemant placed his hand on Priyanshu's shoulders, something he would not have done under ordinary circumstances, neither would he after Priyanshu was announced the director. "Go ahead and take your chance. She doesn't have a boyfriend, otherwise I would have known."

◆

That she was going to Darjeeling for four days to meet a childhood friend soon became known to all at Wellington. Rinita found it hard to control her excitement. Each day seemed to be longer than the previous one. She was happy in real terms after a considerable amount of time, and Priyanshu thought it made a perfect opportunity to place the proposal. And a perfect setting was offered by nature – a clear sky on a full moon night.

That evening during dinner, Priyanshu did something which Rinita thought was very uncharacteristic. He asked Rinita for a coffee outside; the flood of moonlight was too good to waste, he said. Rinita found it poetic and pleasantly amusing.

A pale bluish light had illuminated the mountains, the bushes, the trees and the things which usually remained hidden in the dark of the night. She wanted to thank Priyanshu for the invite, but did not; she saved it for later.

"How is the coffee?" Priyanshu asked kicking off the conversation.

"Lama is a good cook." Rinita wasn't ready to give any credit to Priyanshu for the coffee.

Priyanshu smiled at the smart reply. "So meeting a childhood friend in Darjeeling must be exciting, right?"

"Very," Rinita said with exuberance.

"She is a school friend?"

"We lived in the same village and went to the same school. She lives in London now where her husband is working," Rinita said with the same energy, but her face changed once she realized that she had, out of excitement, divulged more than what was required. The joyous expression changed into a discreet one. But Priyanshu in the dim light failed to notice it, so he continued his enquiry.

"Which village is that?"

"It is a village in Hooghly district. You would not know." Rinita became more careful with her words.

"Isn't it funny that I do not know anything about you even after spending so many days together?" Priyanshu tried to lighten the air.

"What do you want to know?"

Priyanshu spread out his hands in a 'mudra' as if to mean 'anything you want to tell'.

"I come from a very poor family. My father worked in a factory which shut down. He passed away when I was a child. And my mother passed away when I was in college. No siblings, no living relations." Rinita paused. Priyanshu couldn't speak either.

"Will that be all?" she asked.

"I am sorry."

"Don't be. I am not. I am successful and happy…and I am enjoying every bit of the moonlight and every bit of the fresh air. Thank you for the coffee, Mr Agarwal." Rinita sank into the backrest of the chair and spread her arms wide, swayed her head backwards and took a deep breath.

Priyanshu made a swift move into the subject. "And what about marriage?" he asked.

Rinita still had her arms spread out, her face towards the sky and her eyes shut. "No one has proposed to me, Mr Agarwal. If anyone does, I will think about it," she replied without altering her posture.

Priyanshu slipped out of his chair straight on his knees onto the grass beneath Rinita's feet. He pulled out a bunch of roses hastily tied up from behind and held in front of her. "Miss Bose, I am deeply in love with you. Will you consider marrying me?"

Rinita withdrew her arms, opened her eyes and returned to a normal position in no time to find the blue-eyed tall boy kneeling before her with a face dry with anxiety.

"Mr Agarwal, what are you doing?" she exclaimed.

"Exactly what you are seeing, Miss Bose."

"Are you out of your senses?" Rinita almost whispered in an attempt to keep the voice low.

"If it is so, then let it be."

"But this is not possible, Mr Agarwal. Please don't do this."

A dark shadow passed over Priyanshu's face. "Why not Miss Bose?" he could barely ask.

"Because...because of who you are...and who I am. We do not go together."

"I am nobody yet, Miss Bose. You are more successful today than I am."

"Mr Agarwal, please, let us regain our senses; we will discuss this at a convenient time later."

Over the next few days, both Rinita and Priyanshu carefully avoided each other. Both changed their lunch timings to reverse effect, very seldom came face to face except for a weekly management meeting, where Rinita made sure she entered late so that the chairs close to Priyanshu were already taken.

Rinita wanted to keep the big question under the carpet till the Darjeeling trip was over. She was so excited about meeting Chaitali after such a long time that nothing seemed more important than that at that moment. Priyanshu, on the other hand, wanted to give her enough time to consider, reconsider and arrive at an answer which was non-negotiably positive. Also, from what he had learnt about Rinita's past, he knew how important the Darjeeling trip was for her and he wanted her to enjoy it thoroughly.

On Friday afternoon, the day before Rinita was to leave for Darjeeling, Priyanshu dropped into Rinita's chamber. Rinita put up a professional face. Priyanshu was as uncomfortable as her, but he managed to hide it well behind a meticulously revised script.

"So, your leave starts tomorrow?" he asked after taking his seat across the table without looking at Rinita.

"Yep," she replied looking straight at him. She knew from his behaviour over the previous few days that he was as uncomfortable as her, but seeing him talk without being able to make eye contact amused her.

There was a long pause.

"Will you mind if I accompany you to Darjeeling on this trip?" Priyanshu broke the silence with a question which Rinita expected the least.

"Sorry?"

"I can be a good company, I guarantee…and…and…I will not bring up that topic," he said stuttering through the words.

"But it is a very private thing for me, you know."

"I know, but I want to share your joy."

"Well, Darjeeling is open for anyone to visit. You may visit at the same time I am doing. Why do you need my permission?"

"Because I do not want to stay on my own. I do not want to stay far from you."

"Mr Agarwal, please. We are not in a relationship yet," Rinita said unsympathetically.

Rinita wanted Priyanshu to be hurt and back off, but Priyanshu hung on to the word 'yet' which sounded like music to him. Yet means, he thought, there was hope. He reverted with a more emotional tone, "Please Miss Bose, this is the least you could do for me in this situation," he said as if he would cry if she declined.

Rinita took some time to weigh the significance, consequences and risks of having Priyanshu along with her in the trip. Her brain worked quickly and generated a lot of adverse reports.

"How does it work? The last thing I would want is Chaitali to think that you were with me."

"I have a plan. I will manage, don't worry," Priyanshu reassured her.

"No, I want to know the plan in and out. No surprises please."

"Okay." Priyanshu reluctantly started narrating his plan. "You stay with your friends wherever you are booked. I will stay at Planter's Club. We are members there and I have already booked a room. We will bump into each other at the mall or at Glenary's, the two very prominent places where people lost in Darjeeling can be found. You will be surprised to see me there because I came from Kolkata; I wasn't at the garden for the last two weeks. And I will be surprised to see you because I did not know about your vacation plans...."

"It sounds good to me," Rinita interrupted Priyanshu who had more to discuss. Indeed he had done a lot of sensible planning. "From the mall or Glenary's, we will go with the flow." She passed her verdict without showing any interest in hearing the remainder of Priyanshu's plan.

Priyanshu would have agreed to whatever she said. He nodded his head as an obedient student would at the order of his teacher.

The morning fog had still not settled when Rinita and Priyanshu climbed the Wellington owned Gypsy which would drop them to Darjeeling and return.

The Gypsy spiralled through the curves of a hilly road between the forests and occasional tea plantations. The fog was so dense that visibility was cut down to barely three metres. Rinita didn't try to play smart in the presence of Priyanshu. She knew travel in the hilly terrain was scary for the likes of her and murmured prayers for a safe journey.

"I hope we can have breakfast together before parting," said Priyanshu, realizing he was hungry. Rinita didn't answer for some time which made him doubtful whether she was awake and had heard him. "Miss Bose," he called out.

"No, Mr Agarwal, that will be risky. I don't want to take any chances." Priyanshu's heart sank at the heartless reply.

Soon Priyanshu's eyelids, heavy with unfinished sleep gave up and he fell asleep, and neither Rinita nor Priyanshu could enjoy the beauty of the journey. The Gypsy dropped them at their respective destinations: Priyanshu at the Planer's Club and Rinita at the Windamere Hotel.

'Windamere is a fantastic hotel,' Priyanshu had said when he learnt where Rinita was put up. 'It is a heritage hotel which holds on to the old world charm, definitely one of the best in Darjeeling. Your friends have a decent choice.' For some reason, Priyanshu's appreciation of Chaitali's taste made Rinita happy.

Indeed, when Rinita walked into the Windamere with her luggage, she could see and feel what old world charm meant. The heritage building with high ceilings and antique furniture – all in immaculate condition, the smell of wood, the thick carpets and tall fire places made her remember the director's bungalow at Wellington which boasted of the very same 'old world charm' – an interesting expression Rinita had newly learnt, thanks to Priyanshu.

Rinita's room was ready so she checked in, settled her luggage, freshened up and stepped out for a short survey of the city. Chaitali and Abhishek weren't expected before noon. She walked a circle around the observatory hill – the very hill on which the hotel stood and stepped into the open of the famous Darjeeling mall – the highest point of Darjeeling. Finding a Café Coffee Day, Rinita stepped inside and took a comfortable seat by the window. Darjeeling felt colder than Wellington, and a hot tea would be good for acclimatization, she thought.

"Hi." Rinita heard Priyanshu's voice from behind.

"What are you doing here? Are you following me?" she said with her jaws pressed against each other without turning towards him.

Priyanshu felt guilty; he had indeed been following her.

"I forgot to give you my mobile number," he said.

"What will I do with your mobile number? I do not have a mobile phone."

"But still, your friends might."

"Give your card when you meet them. And now go from here. Stop following me. In the evening we will go to Glenary's. Meet us there."

Priyanshu vanished sooner than one could imagine while Rinita ordered a tea and a smoked chicken sandwich.

◆

At around 12.30 there was violent banging on Rinita's door. Rinita immediately knew it could be none other than Chaitali. She rushed to the door and let her in. Chaitali hugged her tightly, and Rinita reciprocated. For some time they did not speak a word, but remained in each other's arms. Both had tears tickling down the corners of their eyes.

After the initial burst of emotion abated, Rinita realized that Chaitali had come straight to her room and had not had a chance to check in, and Abhishek was standing a few steps behind her, waiting for his turn to say 'hi' to Rinita.

Rinita sent both of them packing to their room. They met again at the dining hall for lunch. Chaitali and Abhishek were tired after their nightlong train journey and so was Rinita, having woken up early. They retired to their respective rooms to catch some sleep. "We will have evening tea at Glenary's and it is going to be my treat," said Rinita while parting.

◆

The sun's day job was about to end in less than an hour's time when Chaitali, Abhishek and Rinita stepped out of Windamere into the evening hustle bustle of the Darjeeling Mall. The mall in the evening becomes very crowded, with almost the whole of the tourist community strolling, shopping, riding horses and having refreshments within the vicinity of this small nice open flat land at the top of Nehru Road. The late October temperature of Darjeeling had prompted light winter wear for Rinita, who found Darjeeling colder than Wellington, and none for Chaitali and Abhishek who had come from colder temperatures in London.

Their short walk to Glenary's, which was not further than a few steps down the mall top, faced frequent interruptions from bumping tourists, soliciting vendors of local goodies and the enthusiastic photographer in Abhishek, who, in his own words, was so enthralled seeing Darjeeling after twenty years, that he aimed and clicked at virtually anything and everything he saw.

At Glenary's, a window-side table was arranged. The window offered a rare distinction – something which they realized after occupying the seats, of having the setting sun visible through its left edge and the Kanchenjunga lit in orange through the right.

"It's wonderful, isn't it?" exclaimed Chaitali.

"Yes," responded Rinita. "We must be facing north-west...the directions in thc mountains are so tricky, it is difficult to follow... one twist or spin or one bend around the corner and you are lost... especially on those cloudy-foggy days when you don't have the sun for help."

The direction discussion could have continued for some more time with Rinita eager to cite examples of how difficult it had had been for her to set and follow directions during her initial days at Wellington, had not there been an intervention from behind. "Good evening, Miss Bose. It's so nice to see you here. On a vacation?" asked a male voice and everybody turned to look at it.

Priyanshu stood there in a three piece formal grey suit and a dark blue tie, his hair freshly gelled and spiked, and face shaved not more than an hour ago.

"Oh Mr Agarwal, what a surprise! I am on a vacation to meet my friends. Meet Chaitali, my childhood friend and Abhishek, her better half...and this is Mr Priyanshu Agarwal, a director at Wellington Tea." Rinita had surely practiced the expression of surprise to perfection.

Priyanshu shook hands with both and said unsolicited. "I had come for a planter's meeting which just got over."

"Oh, must be a busy day for you, Mr Agarwal," teased Rinita. "Oh yes," Priyanshu said while pulling out a chair from a nearby table and placing it beside Rinita's.

"But you look rather fresh for a busy day's work."

"Oh yes, that is..." Priyanshu fumbled apprehending Rinita's indications. But soon realizing that nobody had asked him to join the table yet, so he asked, "May I?"

"Well, if you don't have company..." Rinita continued to tease him.

"Of course you can, please do," Chaitali interfered to overrule Rinita.

"Thank you." Priyanshu was indeed thankful to Chaitali for bailing him out.

"But one thing is sure, Mr Agarwal," Abhishek said. "You really do not look like you had a hectic day. Ask my wife how I look after a regular day's job – not better than a dog with a pulled out tongue."

"Also you look too young to be a director," added Chaitali.

Priyanshu wisely picked up Chaitali's question for an answer. "That is the benefit of being born in the promoter's family; you start with the top job," he said.

"Mr Agarwal's father is the Vice Chairman and Managing Director of Wellington Tea," Rinita pitched in with some clarification.

"Oh, I see," said Chaitali. "You look rather humble for one with such rich roots."

Priyanshu smiled shyly and Rinita rounded her eyes at Chaitali who pretended to be flirting.

Over the next one hour, they heard Priyanshu sing elaborate praises of Rinita and her work at Wellington. It was Priyanshu who hosted the tea and muffins and spring rolls and invited them for dinner at the Planter's Club.

"That is so nice of you, Priyanshu. I...I hope I am allowed to call you Priyanshu." Chaitali's pretentious hesitation was directed towards making Rinita jealous, because it had become rather clear by then that there was something brewing between Priyanshu and Rinita – either both were in love with each other or any one was in love and the other was yet to respond.

Abhishek and Chaitali clutched hands under the table, which meant they both had the same understanding of the situation and that they would take the same road ahead.

"By the way, what are you doing tomorrow?" asked Abhishek who went on without bothering to listen to the reply. "We are going to Tiger Hill tomorrow, to watch the sunrise. We will start at four... will pick you up from Planter's."

"First ask him whether or not he has some other plans tomorrow," said Rinita before Priyanshu could respond.

"No-no, I don't have any other plans. I can join you," Priyanshu confirmed hurriedly so as not to give Rinita any opportunity to leave him out.

"Very good, I thought so." Smiled Abhishek.

"By the way, why don't you join us at Windamere? You don't need to stay at Planter's any longer. You are done with your business, right?" asked Chaitali.

"We need to check whether rooms are available. I thought Windamere was fully booked." Rinita made another desperate attempt.

"Of course they have. How could anybody in Darjeeling deny anything to a planter? We will check it out when we return." Abhishek was more confident about a planter's clout in Darjeeling than Priyanshu, the planter himself.

"Great, then let us do something. Let's have a quick dinner here and disperse. We will give Priyanshu the opportunity to host a dinner, but not tonight. We will pick up Priyanshu at four tomorrow morning on our way to Tiger Hill. On our way back, Priyanshu will check out from Planter's and shift to Windamere where we will book a room tonight," Chaitali, like an efficient organizer, spelled out the plan.

"Perfect," confirmed Abhishek.

Priyanshu's expression conveyed that nothing could have been better. And Rinita shrugged her shoulders as if it didn't matter to her.

After dinner, before parting for the day, Priyanshu offered his business card to Abhishek. "I believe knowing each other's mobile numbers will help," he said.

"Oh yes," agreed Chaitali and wrote down her and Abhishek's local mobile numbers on a paper napkin.

"And what about you, Rinita?" Chaitali asked.

"I do not have an active number. Mobiles don't work at Wellington."

❦

At four in the morning, their Scorpio sped towards Ghoom from where it would climb up the road which branched out on the left and ended at Tiger Hill, the spot from where the view of the sunrise was mandatory for anybody who visited Darjeeling.

At Tiger Hill, there was an observatory, inside which all four of them, covered in heavy woollens, had taken their seats. There was still some time for the sun to rise and the seats behind them started to fill up fast. Abhishek adjusted his sophisticated camera to the light and jumped into a fiery mode of clicking with many others once the first rays could be seen in the sky. Chaitali marched up to the edge of the observatory window in support of her husband's photography spree.

Rinita asked Priyanshu "You won't take pictures?" Both of them had stayed away from the crowd.

"I have seen this many times," he said looking firmly into Rinita's eyes. "What I am seeing today cannot be captured by a camera," he concluded.

Rinita knew what Priyanshu meant. She could see the same colours playing on his face, and inside his deep blue eyes.

The crowd had pressed them against each other. Chaitali and Abhishek had moved far in the quest of capturing the colours. Priyanshu's hand pressed against Rinita's, their fingers touched, and Rinita's head rested on his broad shoulders.

◆

As planned, Abhishek had booked a room for the planter, and Priyanshu shifted with his luggage to Windamere that afternoon. After lunch, all four of them took a long walk to the ropeway near North Point. The four-seater suspended glass capsule tilted on either side by turns while crossing the expansive tea gardens from a massive height. Rinita firmly clutched Priyanshu's hands while Chaitali held Abhishek's during the entire course of the round trip which offered spectacular view of the mountains, valleys and tea gardens.

In the evening, the four of them took a shot at bridge. They agreed to remain indoors after a hectic day which had started at three in the morning, and Abhishek suggested bridge not disclosing that he had been a regular at local bridge competitions in India when he lived here and had often been on the winning side. He had adequately trained Chaitali to a level where she wouldn't let his reputation in public falter. They also had practiced the art of reading, like perfect partners in the game – eyes, gestures and secret symbols. A lot of effective communication on strategies, strengths and weaknesses of the hand of the partner happened through such informal modes. They formed a partnership at Windamere too. Rinita was an absolute novice at the game and that she conceded upfront. Priyanshu had played the game a few times with his and his father's friends at the Saturday Club in Kolkata. He knew the rules of the game and agreed to give it a shot with a novice partner. Abhishek elucidated the rules of the game for the benefit of Priyanshu and Rinita. While Priyanshu could re-capitulate the rules and the tricks which he knew and had employed when he had played the game, Rinita found the subject rather difficult for quick assimilation. She relied on Priyanshu who was liberally allowed, for the first few rounds, to advise Rinita on her moves.

They played ten rounds over three hours. The first few ended faster with Rinita struggling to cope up with the finer tricks of the game; but as time progressed, and so did her exposure and experience, she, along with Priyanshu offered more stubborn resistance to the experienced duo.

"Indeed you are a fast learner...hats off to your trainer," said Abhishek to Rinita, pointing at Priyanshu, while arranging the cards back into the case.

Rinita and Priyanshu, with suppressed smiles in silent acknowledgement exchanged glances.

There wasn't an agenda for the next day and fortunately so, because Darjeeling woke up to a gloomy dark rainy day. When Rinita and Priyanshu were woken up by the room service serving bed tea, it was already eight. Rinita lazed for some time lying on her bed and looking at the fir and other trees enveloped by fog and rain through the split of the loosely drawn drapes. She had survived a full monsoon in the mountains, having to pull herself out of bed on such lazy mornings. But at Windamere, she was under no such compulsion; she was free to remain in bed for as long as she wanted. But alas, her hardworking body had forgotten the bliss of indolence. She jumped out of bed and wrapped a shawl around herself. She had the tea and walked out into the lobby to check on the others. She walked past Abhishek and Chaitali's room; a 'Do-Not-Disturb' sign inscribed in clear large font dangled from the handle of the door. She smiled at the sign and walked ahead until she came up to Priyanshu's room and found it partly open. She knocked on the door; a muffled voice asked her to enter. Rinita gently pushed the door to widen the split and peeped inside. She could see a good part of the room – the unmade bed, the steaming tea pot, thrown around night dress, but Priyanshu could not be seen. Out of curiosity Rinita entered the room and started surveying it until she stood in front of the widely open washroom door and saw Priyanshu dressed barely in a towel wrapped around his waist, brushing his teeth with his back to the door. Priyanshu could see a hazy reflection of Rinita on the foggy mirror. Out of natural instinct, he held the knot of his towel with one hand and turned towards Rinita. Rinita, also out of natural instinct, shut her eyes and turned around. But the split second glance at a painstakingly carved out body, private organs concealed behind the towel and the innocent unpretentious look with a tooth brush dangling out of the foamy mouth triggered a strange mixed feeling inside her. The physical attraction was too hard to resist, the naivety too sweet to ignore. But once she was out of the initial abruptness of the situation, Rinita dashed out of the room and broke into loud laughter in the lobby.

Priyanshu hurriedly joined Rinita in the lobby after a while. The shy face, clearly out of the embarrassment of the washroom encounter made her smile. It was she who offered him a toast and scrambled egg breakfast to ease things and soon they were back to normal.

The door to Abhishek and Chaitali's room opened after half past ten. By then, Priyanshu and Rinita had knocked down two coffees, a tea and a heavenly egg-y breakfast.

"Ah," said Abhishek coming up to where Priyanshu and Rinita were seated on cane chairs around a small round tea table against the large window. The glass at the window was blurred from constant hammering of rain drops.

"This is the kind of vacation I always dream of…with nothing to do and nowhere to run. Simply sit back and relax," he said sitting down.

"The weather is so depressing, isn't it?" asked Priyanshu.

"Oh no," protested Abhishek. "If you find this weather depressing, you would die out of melancholy in London. It is like this most of the year."

Priyanshu nodded in agreement.

"I love this weather on holidays, but on other days it's a pain." Rinita took the middle path which none could disagree with.

"By the way friends, you will have to grant us solitude this evening. Today is the anniversary of our first meeting – the commencement of courtship. It is on this date two years ago that I and your dear friend were set up by our families to meet at her place. I had returned from Singapore for a vacation during the pujas without knowing what was being planned behind my back at home," said Abhishek looking at both by turns.

"Nor did I," Chaitali's voice could be heard from behind Abhishek's chair.

"Oh that's lovely…so romantic," said Rinita turning to look at Chaitali.

"And we have planned this vacation carefully to be away from the madness of our homes and relations," added Chaitali while pulling in a chair for herself from a nearby table.

"Solitude granted. Spend the evening the way you had planned. Congratulations to both of you," Priyanshu rose from his chair to shake hands with the couple. "Please excuse me friends. I have some urgent business to attend," he said and dashed out in a hurry.

"What possible business should he have on such a wonderful day?" exclaimed Chaitali.

They glanced at each other but nobody could offer a clue.

◆

It was early evening, and there was a gentle tap on the door. Chaitali had just awakened from a nap while Abhishek was still snoring. She answered the door. A room service boy stood with something elegantly wrapped and ribboned.

"What is this?" she asked.

The boy pointed at a tiny card hanging from the end of the ribbon. Chaitali held the gift which felt like a bottle in her hands and tucked open to read the card. 'To the sweetest couple…from R and P' were the exact words in beautiful calligraphy.

"Thank you," she said, returned to the bed and out of utmost curiosity, unwrapped it without letting Abhishek have a chance to take a look at the wrapping.

In less than fifteen minutes there was vigorous knocking on Rinita's door. Abhishek and Chaitali stood there with a beautiful bottle.

"Piper-Heidsieke Champagne in this part of the world, without any notice…how did you manage?" Abhishek asked at once and his voice reflected the pleasantness of the surprise.

"Virtues of being a planter, sir," was the humble submission from Priyanshu.

"This is the best possible gift I have received in my entire life." Abhishek's eyes glittered while he spoke. "Join us," he urged.

"Thank you, but not today…we have our own little arrangement," Priyanshu said pointing at another similar bottle placed on the study table.

Chaitali went up to Rinita and with both hands pulled her cheeks. "You won't enjoy any less than me, I hope," she said.

A pair of candles flickered at the touch of a burning matchstick in the room deliberately left devoid of any electric illumination. Rinita stooped over the wax sticks with protective palms to ensure the flames got stable. The light waved across her fair skin and pink lips. Priyanshu couldn't take his eyes off what he saw. He wished the clocks would stop ticking, the candles wouldn't burn themselves out, and that the night would never pass. Rinita looked into the deep blue eyes staring intensely at her. The look did not have the tinge of lust she had seen in the eyes of the men she had been with before.

"What?" she asked in a whisper, without taking her eyes off Priyanshu's.

Priyanshu didn't move; he neither blinked nor replied. Rinita raised her brow, her expression asked the question once more, this time without the whisper. Priyanshu slipped down on his knees, once again after the moonlit night at Wellington, this time with a ring in his hand.

"Marry me please." His voice, Rinita thought, had the urge of a child who would want something badly, but wouldn't know why he wanted it. Rinita took her own little time to untangle a few threads of inhibition in her mind. She then lifted her left hand and presented the third finger to Priyanshu. Priyanshu took some time to assimilate his feelings – to realize what he saw was really happening and was not a dream which would die with the wake-up call. He looked up at Rinita again, his eyes moist this time. "Yes," said Rinita as a teardrop trickled down the edge of her eye. Priyanshu slipped the ring on her finger. It fitted perfectly. The diamond sparkled in the candle light as Priyanshu placed his lips across Rinita's; she reciprocated with all her passion.

◆

There was no compulsive reason for Chaitali to not notice the ring on Rinita's finger the next morning at the lobby tea corner. Both were unusually ahead of their male companions and collided with each other in search of a steamy cup at the lobby faintly lit by the golden light of the rising sun. Rinita made no attempt to hide the little sparkling thing when she pulled out her left hand from under the shawl to hold the heavy cup with both hands up to her lips. She noticed Chaitali's keen eyes following her hand movements.

"He proposed?"

Rinita shyly nodded in the affirmative. Chaitali reached out with both hands to clutch Rinita's and bringing them up to her lips, kissed them with a lot of affection.

"He is a lovely man...will make you happy..." she observed. "A memorable day of my life becomes a memorable day for you too."

Abhishek hosted a sumptuous lunch at the Windamere restaurant in honour of the new couple. The multicourse continental menu served with Victorian elegance by white gloved waiters was dotted with regular Chinese dishes to make it more palatable to the Indian appetite. The extravagance of the lunch had something to do, apart from the honest celebration, with paying back in some currency, to Priyanshu, for the exclusive champagne he had gifted them the other night.

In the evening, Rinita and Priyanshu cozied upto one another on the stiff wooden bench on the periphery of the mall, gazing at the streaks of orange painted on the sky by the sun while Chaitali and Abhishek, realizing it was the last day of their vacation, hurried about collecting souvenirs for relatives and friends.

❦

Early next morning, two cars started off from Windamere and parted at Ghoom; one sped towards Wellington Tea and the other towards the Bagdogra airport from where a flight would fly off to Kolkata in the afternoon.

Rinita and Priyanshu decided that Rinita should take off the ring to avoid curious eyes at Wellington and not wear it until the time was appropriate. What was an appropriate time was open for interpretation, but could arguably be considered the ratification by the parents on Priyanshu's side.

Back in Wellington, Rinita and Priyanshu's schedule took off from where it had paused four days back, with both trying hard, too hard at times, to be as normal as they were before. They made it a point not to be seen together in public, smiling, or even exchanging more words than what normal business pleasantries should constitute. The only time Priyanshu and Rinita could spend with each other was the time after dinner when Priyanshu went out into the lawn for a smoke and Rinita for a last look for the day at her man from the closest quarter. During that time of night, they were sure, nobody at Wellington (except Lama, the caretaker of the bungalow) would be awake to witness what the two were up to. Rinita and Priyanshu would spent unmeasured time soaked in love. Sometimes they would talk, sometimes not, but never did they want to let the other leave.

One night in late autumn, while the love birds were out in the lawn, the sky roared, flashed with lightning and broke down with a heavy downpour. Rinita grasped Priyanshu at the sound of the roaring thunder, thrusting her head into his shoulders while the first drops began to fall upon them. Priyanshu could see her face in the flashes of lightening, her eyes shut tight as the cold drops hit against her face. He forgot, in the madness, to rush for shelter under the covered porch of the bungalow barely a few steps away, and instead kissed her on her lips. She kissed back, this time with a bit of tongue.

In no time the rain came down heavily and the temperature took a sharp plunge. Priyanshu, after some struggle had lit a fire at the fireplace of his room and Rinita wrapped a blanket over her naked body stared at him; her wet evening outfit lay on the wooden floor. It was not the first time Rinita was looking at the twitching of the muscles of his bare body, but this time, it wasn't the same eyes; also the vigorous thumping of the heart had not been there the last time around.

Priyanshu, satisfied with the fire, poured two glasses of red wine, offering one to Rinita who remained crouched in one corner of the bed, struggling to hold the blanket tightly enough not to reveal any portion of her bare shoulders. Priyanshu smiled at her plight, realizing she couldn't possibly spare a hand to hold the glass, tilted one delicately into her mouth. The warm taste of sour grapes comforted her and a warm feeling ran from the throat down her body, her senses slightly infringed, her conscience a little shaken. She looked into the deep blue eyes staring naughtily at her; the eyes intoxicated her more than the drink.

Priyanshu ran his fingers down her cheek, over her lips, through the neck, and into the hands holding the blanket closely. Out of some hypnotic effect, Rinita loosened her hands; the blanket dropped to her waist, baring her breasts. Priyanshu continued running his finger over the left breast until it touched the nipple. He employed his other fingers into a cup and caressed her. Rinita had been with men before, but never did she feel such an electrifying urge. She grasped Priyanshu's hand holding her breast and rubbed it against her body. The horse had risen inside Priyanshu and was dying for a ride; his organ protruded pushing against the walls of the thick fabric. Rinita helped him untie his belt and lower his trousers and innerwear; and she put the thick beast inside her mouth. She stroked it gently and licked it vigorously while Priyanshu groaned in partial pleasure and partial impatience.

For a moment Rinita remembered the room, the fire, the drink, and a similar act actioned on Priyanshu's father not many days before. A feeling of guilt had haunted her since she had worn the ring. She knew a day would come when this would happen. She had prepared herself over the days with reasoning to override her conscience. 'It is not a sin and I am not cheating anybody,' she told herself again and again, hoping the sense of guilt would abate.

Soon she was riding on Priyanshu, a posture she had dreamt of in fantasy, a posture in which she was in charge, with full responsibility of a satisfying orgasm on both sides. The beast was uprightly inside her and she stroked it like riding a horse – faster and faster, and faster until her inner walls gushed out fluid in pleasure. After her initial ecstasy settled, Rinita looked back at Priyanshu; his beast was as strong as it was when she had put it in. She thumped harder and deeper and wetter until a warm spray filled her inside. Priyanshu groaned with pleasure, his muscles loosening.

The rest of the night, they lay entangled in each other's arms, hoping to stay so for the rest of their mortal life.

❧

Barely two days had passed after the rainy night when Priyanshu received a message from Kolkata that his mother was unwell and he was required at home. He was in his room packing his belongings when Rinita having heard the news stepped in. Realizing that she did not know much about Priyanshu's mother, she, while helping him fold items of clothing asked, "How is she now?"

"Who, Mom?" Priyanshu responded absentmindedly.

"Hmm..." Rinita confirmed.

"Nothing to worry. It is kind of routine...she has chronic obesity, diabetes and kidney problems. Sometimes things aggravate...a few days in the hospital and then back to normal," Priyanshu replied without any sign of concern or tension.

"How can you remain so cool?"

"You don't know my mother, do you?" Priyanshu's words sounded harsher than they were meant to be. Realizing it might have hurt Rinita, he followed it up with some repair work. "I have seen her for twenty-five years. I know what can go wrong and how it can be set right. Don't worry dear...nothing serious."

Rinita came closer to Priyanshu and placed her head on his shoulders. "When will you be back?"

Priyanshu kissed her on her forehead and promised, "Very soon."

Early morning the next day, after the luggage had been loaded and it was time for Priyanshu to start, his eyes met the reddened eyes of Rinita who had stayed awake all night, sitting at the corner of her bed, praying for a swift recovery of Priyanshu's mother. A faster recovery guaranteed a faster return for Priyanshu. Priyanshu touched her fingers but neither could speak. Chetri turned on the ignition and the car rolled away. Priyanshu and Rinita didn't lose eye contact until the vehicle disappeared into the early morning fog.

◆

The first message in her official mailbox, that Rinita found while going through the daily routine of mails the next morning was from Priyanshu. 'Reached safely. Things will take some time. May not be reachable always. Will return soon. Love, Priyanshu.' Must have been sent from his mobile, she thought while recalling instances when Priyanshu had been lazy to type long sentences on his mobile, also in official mails. She smiled to herself.

Barely an hour later, the telephone rang. Rinita's eyes glittered, her heart beat faster in anticipation of hearing his voice. She looked at her reflection on the glass surface of the office desk to ensure she looked nice. She whispered into the mouthpiece, "Hello."

"Hello…hello…Rini, it's me…do you recognize me?" A hesitant male voice said.

Rinita's heart sank with disappointment. "No I don't," she replied inhospitably, making it clear that she wasn't interested.

"It's me…Mahesh…you don't recognize my voice?"

Rinita didn't want to speak to anybody except Priyanshu, but she couldn't hurt Mahesh. "Of course I do dear. But it is unexpected, isn't it, that's why it didn't occur to my mind," she said in a tone like she would talk to a child.

"Okay okay, that's why. I was wondering how Rini could forget my voice. I rechecked the number Chaitali gave me."

The answer to Rinita's next question was already obtained. Chaitali shouldn't have, she thought. This number was supposed to remain secret. But unlike Souvik, Chaitali did not know the gravity of the situation. I will have to call her up and ask her not to share it with anybody else, she decided.

"So how are you Rini?... Not been in touch for so long. Are you angry with me for some reason?" Mahesh exhibited his characteristic innocence.

"No dear, how can I be angry with you? It is only that my new job is so demanding I hardly get time to call my friends."

"You work on Sundays also?"

"Sundays and holidays."

"That's bad. Tell your boss that you need some time to talk to your best friend."

"Of course I will."

"Chaitali was saying that it is time Rini should settle down."

"Oh, is it?"

"Yes, I didn't tell her the secret."

"What secret?"

"That I have asked you to marry me and you have said yes."

Rinita felt sorry at Mahesh's naivety; he had taken seriously some words spoken by Rinita casually at some forgotten moment. The news of her engagement with Priyanshu would have to be broken very carefully, she thought. For the time being, she would let him live with his treasured dream.

"Good that you didn't tell her. Imagine the fun we will have when she will get the surprise."

There was silence for a while. "Okay Mahesh, nice talking to you. Will talk at length later. I will have to get back to work." Rinita wanted to end the conversation; she couldn't lie anymore.

"Okay…but listen…one thing…don't share my number with anybody or tell anybody anything about me, okay?"

"Oh sure, if you say so. Goodbye."

"Goodbye dear." Rinita sank into the comfort of her revolving chair, feeling sad that she would have to hurt the purest person she had known. Given a choice she would not want to do that, but Priyanshu was not a choice any more, but an irresistible compulsion.

The anxiously awaited call had not come and seven days had passed. Rinita tried calling Priyanshu's mobile, but it seemed to be 'unreachable' every time. Rinita got worried, but she didn't want to show a lot of interest, lest it raise any suspicion. She had full faith in Priyanshu that he would not spend a moment more than what was absolutely necessary away from her.

On the eighth day, Wellington had a visitor it least expected – Senior Labour Officer Joydeep Sarkar. He dropped in without any intimation and also without any fixed or burning agenda, at least apparently. There was no labour trouble – no demands, no charters, no agitation, no loss of production – nothing at all. On the contrary, terms of the management with the workers had never been smoother. The reason for his arrival at the garden soon became a subject of speculation and his arrival an unwelcome inauspicious indication to many, because Joydeep Sarkar had seldom paid a visit to the garden over the last three years, including times of hostile labour unrest.

As the Junior Labour Officer directly reporting to Joydeep, Rinita had become his shadow in all his meetings throughout the day, but in none she found any valuable issue being discussed. Towards evening, during a tea break, she asked him directly, not being able to contain her curiosity. “We will talk in the evening. Come to my room at eight. I have been put up in the MD’s room,” came the reply.

As an obedient subordinate, Rinita knocked the door of the MD’s room sharp at eight. Rinita momentarily hesitated to enter the room which till eight days back had been occupied by the blue-eyed lean young man. Joydeep was sitting on the bed with some files and papers scattered around; the same bed on which Rinita had spent an unforgettable night. He joined her on the sofa in a way in which no direct eye contact was possible. Rinita found the sitting positions rather strange. She preferred to remain mute. She was keener to understand whether the purpose of his visit was caused by any failure on her part to discharge her duties.

Rinita expected Joydeep to start the conversation with the reply to the question she had asked during the tea break early in the evening, but Joydeep did not utter a word. He carried a file in his hand which he remained busy browsing. Rinita thought of making a start. “So what brought you here?” she enquired again.

Joydeep cleared his throat as a speaker would do before starting a speech, and said without lifting his eyes from the file, “It is not work related.”

“Then what?” asked Rinita to cut short another long pause.

“It is a personal matter which I have been asked to take care of by Mr Agarwal.”

Rinita began making possible guesses. At one point she got a bit tensed imagining that the personal thing could be regarding her and Priyanshu.

But Joydeep having got started, didn’t waste much time in getting to the point, proving Rinita’s fear to be true.

"You can imagine how important a matter like marriage is for a Marwari business family."

It was not a question and Rinita didn't offer a reply. She held her breath anxiously to hear more.

"Priyanshu is the only child for the Agarwals, who want him to marry a lady within their community, preferably from a business family of equal standing, someone whom they would choose for him."

Rinita had shut her eyes, put her hands together with fingers interlocked and prayed silently to the almighty so that he may make Joydeep speak some hopeful words about her relationship with Priyanshu.

Joydeep continued, "They had a beautiful young lady in mind with whom they had almost finalized his marriage long back when he was in America."

Rinita continued praying, though her confidence that god could make a turnaround gradually faded.

"Not that Priyanshu did not know about this...he had met the girl more than once, but had neither approved, nor disapproved of the proposal."

He paused and turned to take a look at Rinita whose eyes were shut. Joydeep somewhere inside felt pity for the poor girl whose dreams he was assigned to shatter.

"But since Priyanshu had come to Wellington, his family had observed some changes in his behaviour which alarmed them about his marital intensions. And very recently, from reliable sources, they had come to know about a sort of romantic engagement between yourself and him..."

Joydeep took a deep breath and continued, "which they do not approve."

Rinita opened her eyes.

"They have warned Priyanshu that he would be deprived of his inheritance if he dishonors their wishes in this matter...he will be disowned as the son of Mrs and Mr Prem Agarwal."

"Wait a minute...what does Priyanshu have to say about it?" Rinita spoke and spoke with aggression.

"Priyanshu hasn't seen the real world. He failed to perceive the fallout of the threat," Joydeep replied calmly.

"What does that mean? He still insists that he wants to marry me, right?"

"Yes, he does," Joydeep replied hesitantly.

"Then what is this discussion all about? It is his decision and he has taken it."

"Mr Agarwal wants you to turn him down." Joydeep hit the crux of the discussion.

"Why should I do that?" Rinita almost panted in excitement.

"Because you definitely do not want Priyanshu to know about your past...and what your real job in Wellington has been." Joydeep pronounced the words he thought would be impossible for him to speak to a lady. He had countered Mr Agarwal saying that he wasn't the right choice of person for this job, but in vain."

"Oh...so you are blackmailing me?" Rinita jumped up and stood in front of Joydeep. Her face had turned red with anger.

"If that is how you take it," Joydeep looked at her in the eyes, but retained his cool.

"You...you pimp, how dare you come to me with such a proposal?" she shouted.

"Cool down, Miss Bose, even the walls have ears." Joydeep stood up to stand face to face with his mission.

"And what if I tell Priyanshu the truth myself? Then he will decide."

"Priyanshu in all possibility will not sleep with someone who has slept with his father." Joydeep knew he had to be rude. He had to inflict pain on the poor girl.

"You know what? He already did...on the very bed on which you will sleep tonight."

"Then I stand corrected. Let me rephrase it. Priyanshu will not sleep again with someone who has slept with his father. Does it make sense now?" Joydeep expressed no surprise at the newly discovered reality.

"Miss Bose," the seasoned labour officer softened his tone. "Please do not misunderstand me," he continued. "You may call me a pimp or whatever...But I have been assigned a task, and being in his employment I cannot say 'no'. I have a sister of your age... trust me, my regard for you is no less. Mr Agarwal is not a saint, but yes, he pays your bills, and mine too. And he paid your bills at a time when you were in difficulty – without a job and with a fear for your life. Should all that be forgotten for love?"

Joydeep ambled across the room with his right hand stuck inside the cupped palm of the other, a sign he often made, when he was in the middle of making a deal.

Rinita continued to shiver out of anger but she paid a patient hearing, partly because none of the words spoken by Joydeep were untrue and partly because she became impatient to see where it was all headed to.

After a reasonable wait for a reaction from Rinita, Joydeep continued, "Try to conceive the broader picture, Miss Bose. Leave aside the question of community and social standing and the cliché of parents choosing a bride of their liking for their son. You are heading for a situation where you have slept with your father-in-law and your husband doesn't know about it, whereas your mother-in-law, knowing her husband's character well enough will take no time to guess it."

Joydeep took a calculated pause to read Rinita's reaction. He found Rinita's shivering had reduced, her face had turned pale and her head had dropped. She seemed to have lost the strength to stand; she could drop on the floor any time, he feared. But he had to hammer the iron he had spent so much effort in heating. "And you wish to lead a happy married life with a loving husband and consorting in-laws. How long Miss Bose, how long do you think this lie can survive?"

Rinita couldn't utter a word; her face pointed down in sorrow and shame. Tears emerged out of her eyes and dropped near her feet on the wooden floor.

"This will not leave anybody happy, Miss Bose…ask your conscience, is this what you want?"

Joydeep's question pierced Rinita in the middle of her chest, as if someone had aimed an arrow at her. It pained, it bled, but Rinita still had some courage left to want to know. "What do you want me to do?"

Joydeep was relieved to hear the question.

"Mr Prem Agarwal is immensely thankful for your contribution at Wellington. He would prefer a ceremonious parting. He is deeply pained to acknowledge the heartbreak the separation would cause to you, especially on the matter of Priyanshu. As a token of thanks for your sacrifice and kind gesture, he has sent this," Joydeep pulled out an envelope and handed it over to Rinita.

Rinita could barely hold the envelope with her vigorously shaking hand and pull out what was inside – a cheque of twenty-five lakhs written in her name.

Her face changed from pale to red again as she looked at the cheque. But instead of an angry outburst, she laughed out loud. Mixed emotions: anger, sorrow, despair expressed in laughter.

"So, Mr Agarwal is hell-bent on making an expensive whore out of me," she said with her eyes fixed on the cheque. "Who on earth could charge such a sum for a blowjob which doesn't bring an erection."

Her laugh aggravated, became almost hysterical; by the time she could rein her laughter, tears gushed out of her eyes.

Joydeep said nothing, it wasn't a time to speak for him; he had to give her the opportunity to vent the pain and insult.

"Where is Priyanshu? How much does he know about this shit?" she asked after a gathering herself.

"Priyanshu has gone back to America after a fight with his parents."

"What?" she exclaimed in disbelief.

"Why not? He has a multi-entry visa. And it is a place where he can escape the realities he faces here."

Rinita remained silent, Priyanshu's whereabouts shouldn't bother her any more.

"But he will be back…to you…for you. I have known him for years," Joydeep said without any provocation. He knew his prediction could send a ray of hope to Rinita and riding on the optimism she might refuse the deal altogether. But still he took a chance. She deserved one kind gesture.

"That is why Mr Agarwal wants you to use that money as an investment in a new life at a new place far from where his search could take him," he added.

Rinita slipped the cheque inside the envelope and placed it on the file. "It is a big deal, Mr Sarkar. I need time to deliberate," she said with certainty.

"Tomorrow morning at eight, same place?" he suggested.

"I prefer the lawn at tea time. Fresh air is good for deals." She turned to leave the room.

"Please forgive me for doing this."

Rinita turned to Joydeep with an advice, "Don't be apologetic for what you knowingly do." She slammed the door shut.

Bright sunshine flooded the lawn, and clusters of white cloud floated in the sky while Rinita looked through her oversized shades at the lush magnificent plantations of Wellington Tea Estate, her home for a short but memorable part of her life. The brownish tinge of her shades – which she had worn to hide the tired weepy eyes from the world – brought a gloomy effect to the beauty of Wellington. Each tree, each grass blade, each leaf, she felt, mourned with her at her loss of love.

Joydeep joined her sharp at eight and soon tea was served. He was in shades too but for a different reason altogether – he didn't want his eyes to reflect any momentary weakness which might fail the purpose. The two of them positioned face to face across the table with no possibility of direct eye contact made a perfect setting for an arms-length deal to be professionally negotiated.

"So where are we?" he started, lifting the cup meant for him, without a customary morning greeting.

"How did the news of our romance reach the Agarwal household?" Rinita returned the question with another. She had thought hard all night, but couldn't identify possible suspects.

"Does it really matter?"

"To me, it does."

"I don't think it is important anymore."

"Then I don't think we need to discuss this anymore." Rinita made no effort to hide her discontent.

"On a rainy night both of you were seen kissing each other," Joydeep felt embarrassed to describe a private act.

"And who saw that?" Rinita's question was as direct as she meant it to be.

"Mrs Dutta, the manager's wife. She happened to come out into the lawn to bring in the clothes left in the open for drying." Joydeep sighed.

"Oh I see." Rinita's face showed no special expression at the discovery.

"So can we get back to business?" Business indeed, Joydeep smiled at himself. He was eyeing the position of a Senior Vice President if he successfully pulled it through.

"What is the say of Mrs Agarwal in the Agarwal household?" was her next question.

"Totally out of context," Joydeep said frowning.

"Not to me." Rinita maintained her cool.

"How does it matter?"

"Just wanted to understand, in a conservative Marwari household how does it matter what Mrs Agarwal guesses or discovers?"

"Because Wellington will come as an inheritance to Priyanshu from his mother's side. You would remember Mr Agarwal is the Managing Director cum Vice Chairman at Wellington. Any guesses who the Chairman is?"

"Hmm..." The picture got clearer to Rinita. How little she knew about the Agarwals, she thought.

"Any more questions?"

"No...back to business.

"So..." Joydeep reminded Rinita that it was her turn to comment on the offer.

"Oh my turn, is it?" she sounded naïve. "Let me make a counter offer."

Joydeep was taken aback at the statement. How soon could she forget her love and trade it for money?

"I know what you are thinking," said Rinita with a sarcastic smile. "What a whore she is, talking about money in exchange of love."

"No no, not that." Joydeep was shocked.

"Must be, Mr Sarkar. I have slept with enough men to know what they might be thinking. But let me remind you that it was you who came to me with a cheque. I did not go to you begging for money. I am only playing the game as per the rules set by you. So why fuss?"

"Place your terms." Joydeep realized it would be utterly foolish to underestimate the lady he had set out to deal with.

" Fifty lakhs."

"Good heavens...do you realize how much money that is?" Joydeep deliberately exaggerated his reaction.

"Well, if you can't afford it, then we can call it off." Rinita remained stern.

"What do you stand to gain if it is called off?" This time it was Joydeep's turn to get excited.

"Nothing," she said indifferently.

"Do you know how powerful these people are?" Joydeep used the dice he had saved for the last.

"Ah, there you are showing your true colours. I know they are very powerful. They can kill me and bury my body somewhere under this vast plantation. Lot of land to hide a tiny body like mine, right?" she said smirking.

"What do you mean?" asked Joydeep.

"What I mean is I have friends who know about me and Priyanshu...and if I disappear or die, they will fight it out for me."

Her words sounded shrill to Joydeep who had by then run out of ammunition.

"Is that all?" Joydeep thought of confirming before he proceeded with the next step.

"That will be all," Rinita said and laughed at Joydeep's helplessness.

"Okay, give me an hour. I need to discuss it with Mr Agarwal. Let's gather exactly after an hour." He stood up to return to his room.

"Tell Mr Agarwal," said Rinita, "if the deal is through, he can get a blowjob for free." She burst out in laughter.

◆

Not even half an hour had passed when there was a tap on Rinita's door. Rinita invited Joydeep inside, but finding him hesitant, she assured him saying, "Don't worry, I won't shout rape." Joydeep spent no time in jumping in; he knew it was not at all safe to talk to her in the hallway.

"Fifty is done. Do you need cash?"

"Nope. Two cheques, one in my name and the other blank. I will fill it in. I hope they don't bounce, because if they do, I will be back," she warned.

"Good, you will get the cheques by this evening. The accountant will sign them for you."

"Thank you. I will hand over my resignation then. Kindly make arrangements to drop me to the airport tomorrow morning. I will be ready by then." Joydeep found Rinita surprisingly cool, devoid of any emotion.

"There is one more thing I almost forgot," said Rinita. Joydeep curiously looked back. "The free blow job…Did you tell him that?" she asked with a serious expression. Joydeep dashed out of the room to save himself from further embarrassment.

◆

It was a depressingly cloudy morning and the Gypsy in which she had arrived at the garden at the fall of summer waited to take her far away from Wellington. Rinita had sent a message to Hemant to be present at the time of her departure. With her luggage loaded, it was time to say goodbye. Joydeep made it a point to wake up early to wish her luck, or maybe to ensure she was really gone.

Hemant stood before the car, bearing a grim-but-not-curious look as if he knew that there was a love story and that it would not succeed. Rinita walked up to him. "You know everything, don't you?" she asked. Hemant nodded.

"You won't say anything?" she asked.

"You two would have made a beautiful pair. But the Agarwal family is not a place where you should spend the rest of your life. You are destined to fly in the sky like a butterfly. I wish you well for your future. May you find love and success," he said in a single breath as if he wouldn't have been able to hold on to tears had he taken a break.

"I don't have the time to say goodbye to Mini and Varsha. All of you have been so kind." Her voice chocked while she spoke. She pulled out an envelope from inside her handbag and handed it to Hemant.

"Open it after I am gone," she said and climbed the Gypsy. Hemant shut the door for her and watched it speed away till it disappeared into the morning fog.

Hemant opened the envelope and emptied its contents on his other hand. There was a cheque of twenty-five lakhs in the name of 'Wellington Tea Private Limited – Employees Welfare Fund'. There was a letter written on a Wellington official letter pad with Rinita Bose's name imprinted at the top. The handwritten letter meant to serve as a covering note to the cheque carried the following words:

Dear Hemant,

Please deposit this cheque to the Employees Welfare Fund a/c. The amount is to be used exclusively for construction/ renovation of the school and medical centre and for their maintenance and necessary supplies.

Thanks

Rinita.

Hemant's vision blurred while he looked up into the sky; tears he had fought so hard to hold back began streaming out.

PART 3:
Shahid Khan, Abhishek Chatterjee and Mahesh Jha

Rinita unmindfully kept on rotating the diamond ring on her left ring finger with the thumb and the index finger of the right hand while the early morning breeze blowing across her from the window of Borivali-Churchgate local disarranged her hair. There wasn't a lovely view outside the window – no greenery, no touch of nature, only buildings and slums. Rinita preferred the window seat with her back towards the front of the train. On the one hand, it would be far from the madding crowd, and on the other, the breeze wouldn't directly blow into her. But very often than not, she couldn't manage this strategically demanding seat as there were other takers; competition was stiff.

Rinita, partly out of habit and partly because she sat window-side, always carried a light stole to wrap around as a protection against any kind of seasonal mischief. More than the discomfort of the cool breeze it was falling sick that she was worried about, something she could not afford having invested a lot of money – two-and-a-half lakhs to be precise in the most famous and expensive acting school in India. The school owned and run by a successful veteran Bollywood actor boasted of illustrious alumni.

Rinita always had a Bollywood dream. She had grown up on Bollywood movies and her favourite daytime fantasy was that she was being driven away in an expensive foreign brand luxury car while hordes of fans were running after it in the hope of catching a glimpse.

The money from the Wellington account which she had kept for herself had presented her with the opportunity to give it a try. Though a part of her chest still pained whenever she thought of the price she had to pay for it. A drop or two would invariably tickle down, on a sleepless night, on the pillow whenever she remembered Priyanshu's dreamy blue eyes. She did not know how Priyanshu had reacted to her disappearance, or what evils about her his well-wishers might have told him. Perhaps Priyanshu was told that it was her who had blackmailed them for money and Priyanshu might have trusted those lies without suspicion. If her past wasn't tainted the way it was, she would definitely not have given up on her love so easily. However, she knew she had to move on.

Finding a paying guest accommodation at a cheaper suburb along the western line of the Mumbai suburban railway network wasn't difficult. It didn't take Rinita more than seven days of careful read of the classifieds and a couple of physical inspections to zero-in upon the Borivali apartment she currently shared with two more girls – a struggling model from somewhere in Punjab and an advertising professional from Lucknow.

Luckily, Borivali acted as a terminal station for suburban trains plying to Churchgate. Anybody who liked to board empty trains preferred terminal stations. The reason for which Rinita chose that place at the edge of the Mumbai suburban map as her home was precisely the same. A wise decision for someone who was in show business, as smelly, sweaty, tired faces, crushed clothes and melted makeup could never make a good day. Nor impression.

There was nothing to look at outside the window. The only thing she would do during her twenty minute journey from Borivali to Andheri was either to listen to music on the FM or from the playlist of her android phone, or to rehearse in her mind what she had learnt the previous day. In both cases, one constant factor would be her unmindfully playing with the ring, the ring which she had never worn while at Wellington, but religiously worn since she arrived in Mumbai. The purpose was to repel unsolicited suitors by indicating a presently active romantic engagement.

There were other constants too, among which the most interesting was a young man with unkempt long hair and a full beard, always, either scribbling or reading on and from a bunch of papers arranged in a flat file. He boarded and de-boarded, just like Rinita, at Borivali and Andheri, and always took the seat against the window opposite to her.

Rinita's classes started at eight with a mandatory fitness session for all. On her first day at the school, Harsh Patel, the legendary Bollywood actor and founder chairman of the school, in his welcome speech had emphasized the importance of fitness for all (across disciplines) and a toned body for aspiring actors in lead roles in particular. The heavily equipped gym had enough machines for everyone. While cardio and freehand was fun, Rinita initially struggled with weights. The pain inflicted on her calves, thighs and shoulders after the first few days of workout gave her a nightmare. She thought of bunking a few days' classes so that she could get the pain to subside. But two reasons deterred the bunking decision: one was the handsome gym instructor's warning that a break would mean a new start and new pain, and the other was the notional loss in terms of price per class which would go unrecovered for every missed class.

Thankfully all meals except dinner was included in the course fees which relieved Rinita of arranging the kind of fat-free salt-free diet the school nutritionist had prescribed for wannabe actors. At dinner, she shared boiled vegetables and two slices of bread – devoid of any butter or jam – with her model room-mate, while the advertising executive, according to her with sincere feeling of guilt, polished off a full square vegetarian dabba every evening. 'Conviction is the investment to success.' Rinita recited her mantra whenever her mouth watered at the flowing aroma of palak paneer, mustard bhindi or dal tarka.

Rinita wasn't in the best of moods. The previous evening, she had had a difficult time reproducing a particular sound the voice-and-diction instructor insisted was necessary to make any sense out of the Urdu word in question. That the Bengalis were traditionally poor in their Hindi/ Urdu accent was no valid excuse. She had to, she knew, overcome the impediment if her Bollywood dreams were to be remotely realized. Absent in thoughts of the Urdu fiasco, Rinita did not notice when the train reached and halted at the Andheri station. She suddenly noticed that the full beard had disappeared and his seat had been taken over by a teenage girl. Rinita jumped onto her feet and dashed out of the train in a hurry, in the process losing her balance and toppling on the full beard from behind. The poor fellow tripped over, his file flew out of his grasp and its loose contents dispersed all around. Rinita fell on top of him, and her book on method acting landed some five feet away. The hasty crowd de-boarding the train exercised enough caution not to stamp the stationery, but beyond that offered little respect. The unkempt hair reached out for the loose papers with exceptional urgency. Rinita, realizing the papers must be of immense value to the owner, joined him in their re-collection. By the time they managed to get all the papers together, the platform had emptied itself of the overflowing crowd. Rinita rolled her eyes through some of the sheets she had collected. They contained scribbled notes, sketches and words arranged in form of, what she thought, was a play.

"I am so sorry. It is all because of me," Rinita said to the man who sadly inspected the torn sheets.

Few moments had passed when he realized that Rinita wouldn't move without her apology being accepted. So he looked up and replied, "It's okay...happens. Typical Mumbai insensitivity...can't complain."

He thought Rinita would be content with his reply, but Rinita stayed on conversing. "Is this a play or something?" she asked.

"It is a screenplay," he replied with reluctance.

"Oh, Hindi?'

"Yes."

"Movie or tele."

"Movie."

"You have written it?"

He drew his right arm out and introduced himself. "Shahid Khan, director, screenplay writer."

"Oh, glad to meet you. I am Rose."

"Actress, I suppose?"

Rinita looked at the book on method acting she held in her hand. "Aspiring," she said.

"Me too...though I have done a short film and a documentary. No luck with movies so far."

Rinita referred to her watch, the Longines gifted by Arindam which she never stopped wearing despite the cruel memories it carried. Arindam's watch and Priyanshu's ring both harmoniously coexisted within close proximity of each other, both carrying strong and painful reminiscences of her past from which she drew strength to face the world with increased courage and conviction to live and live well. She had the right, she claimed, like anybody else to live a life happy and successful.

"Oh, I am late!" she exclaimed. "I need to rush. Glad to meet you. See you again." She hurriedly wrapped up the conversation. Shahid barely got the opportunity to say 'goodbye'.

Breathless at twelve km/ hr. on the treadmill, a strange question struck her. Why did she introduce herself as Rose to Shahid? Very strangely, it was the first time she had hidden her real identity. Did she do it on purpose or out of mistake? Maybe a slip of tongue or an unprepared reaction to a certain setting?

Her mind worked hard untangling the reason. Rinita had enrolled in the acting school with her original name. But in his inaugural speech Harsh had asked those who wanted to be known by a screen name, to decide on the preferred names before their resume, along with portfolio albums, were sent out to various production houses. "You need to hit the market with a hundred and ten percent of preparation. Finalize your name, looks and goals," he said.

Many years ago, at Chaitali's house in Phoolbari village, taking advantage of her parents' trip to attend a relative's wedding, the three musketeers watched with extraordinary enchantment, a Hollywood movie on television – *Titanic*. Both the ladies had wept heartily at the sorrow of the lead female protagonist Rose, especially at her survival at the expense of love. Mahesh, not having too much emotion to share, and having known Rinita's harboured dreams of becoming an actress, made an innocent prophecy instead – that Rinita would make a Rose someday. "That makes sense," remarked Chaitali while still very much in the grip of sympathy for the screen Rose.

"Your name is Rinita Bose. If you merge them into a meaningful abbreviation, it becomes R-OSE."

Rinita had decided on her screen name the day Harsh had made the speech, but had never used it until the moment she introduced herself to Shahid Khan. Must be a good omen, she thought.

What had started in winter happened to ripen by the advent of spring – in terms of her acting classes as well as her budding friendship with Shahid Khan, who with time, would become her most trusted friend in an unknown city.

Shahid being a struggler of limited means from a smaller town of Kanpur never had the luxury of attending a fashionable acting school. His normal reaction towards Rinita, who was slightly more resourceful in comparison, was expected to have been of natural animosity; but on the contrary, Shahid treated her with genuine tenderness. Rinita never divulged enough of her past, but Shahid's creative eyes read a reflection of a suppressed sorrow. 'A thousand untold stories' was what Shahid told his close confidant and associate Munna about what he saw in Rinita. She, on the other hand, found in him a friend who was different from the people she met in school or in an audition – someone who was willing to help and guide and didn't seem to have romance in mind. She had been slightly tentative initially, until she met Fatima, Shahid's school teacher fiancée at an Andheri coffee shop, and thought they made a sweet couple.

Shahid helped her with all that she struggled with in school – method acting, Urdu, voice and diction, film history and world classics to name a few. The subjects where she needed no help wasn't a short list either: dance, dressing, make-up, styling, fitness and diet, and dinner table manners were topics in which either she had some previous knowledge or acute interest.

It soon became a regular feature to spend Saturday evenings at Shahid's place – a small rented flat in an old partly dilapidated building in Borivali East. Shahid's modestly decorated apartment boasted of a modern home theatre set-up, in which, picking out of his enormous collection of world classics, Shahid played those which he thought was a must watch for any student of cinema. It was in Shahid's den that Rinita was introduced to the form of cinema she had for so long been oblivious to – *Bicycle Thief, Eight and a half, Vertigo, Rashomon, Wild Strawberries* and a lot more. Fatima, not having a lot of interest for cinema made herself useful in the kitchen. The scrumptious aroma of kebabs and biriyanis flowing out of the kitchen into the living room was often a distraction to the attentive audience comprising Rinita and Munna. Not that Rinita always understood all the cinematic masterworks she saw, or those Shahid explained, but she started liking the flavour of those films.

While trees found new leaves and humidity returned in the air, Rinita got busy running from one audition to another with a carefully compiled portfolio of stills, video recordings of her performances at school and the modelling adverts she had done way back in Kolkata. Shahid continued his persevered search for a producer who would share his excitement about his ambitious new project, which was, in Shahid's words, a big budget serious cinema – a combination which made it a remotely attractive proposition.

"Why would you like to work with such an audacious subject?" Rinita once asked Shahid rather naively.

"I don't know why, but ever since I've read this book, I can't get it out of my mind," he said.

Rinita found the reasoning rather strange since neither the author was known nor did the book make it to the bestseller list. It was a self-published book which, Rinita discovered after further enquiry, Shahid had come to know about it from Facebook and had spent a few hundreds to buy from Amazon. The book was titled *The Obituary of Salim Nabi,* and dealt with a Muslim young man from Mumbai who unknowingly sheltered a terrorist and had to prove his patriotic credentials by helping the probe.

Shahid looked unusually serious, Rinita thought, when he said, "The story talks about the likes of us."

"I don't think it will have songs or dances or an expensive cast...then why should it be a big budget movie?" Rinita asked hesitantly.

"Ah, you can't think outside the formulae, can you?" Shahid's counter question was definitely an expression of disappointment with his pupil. But he went ahead to explain in lucid terms: "It shows the prime minister, some other ministers, army officers and their offices. It needs to be shot in London, Delhi, Mumbai, Goa, Rishikesh and you know where else?"

As expected, Rinita presented a blank look.

"Siachen glacier," he continued, "...also we need fighter aircrafts, Mercedes Benz...and have a visually convincing army and civilian crowd," Shahid paused as Rinita seemed flabbergasted at the list.

"Do you think all these come cheap?" Shahid resumed his explanation.

"The two line brief you had given me about the story doesn't give the idea that so many things would be necessary," Rinita said rather sheepishly.

"You should read the book to understand it better. It is a protest against a lot of stereotypes. I flew down a couple of times to Kolkata to work on the script with the author. Do you think it is all that easy?"

Shahid pulled out from inside his file a dull looking book. Rinita accepted it with reluctant humility and flipped through a few pages. The margins had scribbles in tiny, almost illegible handwriting.

"It contains my notes. It will help you get to the depth of the story," Shahid said with an air of pride. Rinita randomly read a chapter called 'Goa 2' in which Kirti kisses the protagonist Salim on the lips. There was something of interest for her, she assumed.

Rinita's acting videos didn't quite impress the producers and casting directors she could gain access to, but the dance clips – especially the ones in which she had danced in revealing outfits to popular Bollywood item numbers – managed to grab some eyeballs. No wonder she loved modern Bollywood dancing which required nothing more than fitness and some display of sensuality.

One kind lady casting director took her to a corner one day and gave her a valuable suggestion. "I am not saying you won't make a good actor," she said, "...nobody knows when success comes and how...but I suggest keep on trying for dancing as well as you have a natural flair for it."

There were two ways one could have reacted to the unsolicited tip – to sink into depression on the thought that chances of success in acting was bleak, or to be happy at the compliment and take the advice seriously. Rinita was an eternal optimist type, thus, she chose the latter. She made it a point to include the choreographer's offices in her regular job search hops, and within a fortnight landed with a minor assignment of dancing in a ladies group behind the leading lady in a movie. The leading lady, she came to know, was Priyanka Chopra. She got goose bumps at the very thought of sharing screen space with one of the top-most heroines in her very first assignment.

Rinita called Shahid straight from the choreographer's office in Santacruz to give him the good news. "Where are you?" he sounded excited, "...I will be in Khar in half an hour's time. Take an auto-rickshaw and come to the Khar station...wait outside the East gate. I will meet you there. Then, we will celebrate," he said.

At the Khar station, Munna arrived first and then Shahid, and together they went to meet a one-time famous and currently wanting-to-make-a-comeback producer who had shown more interest in Shahid's ambitious script than anybody else. Vasant Dariyanani, the veteran Sindhi producer of more than ten blockbuster movies in the late eighties had been out of action due to near bankruptcy in his diamond export business. He had been longing for some time to make a serious comeback into the industry and had been looking for the right project.

"But, it's a cruel place, you know; you are valued as long you are flying from one success to another. Once you are out, nobody will care for you," Shahid said in a voice dipped in hopelessness.

"And knowing all this, we are trying to make a place for ourselves over here," Rinita shared the misery.

Shahid took a deep breath while guiding the rickshaw up to the doorstep of Vasant Dariyanani's office.

A secretary made them sit in the lobby while Mr Dariyanani got ready for the meeting.

Rinita leaned to whisper a cruel question into his ears. "But why should he produce Salim Nabi? Your movie will not make good business," she asked.

Shahid, by then, had become so habitual of all her naivety that he didn't mind the unpleasantness of the subject.

"Because he doesn't have a team or any infrastructure...he needs a director who will take all the headaches for him. And no established director or actor will take the risk of working with him in this situation," he explained

"Oh!" Rinita exclaimed as she always did after learning something new.

Vasant Dariyanani, a thin, fair man in his seventies, with scanty hair and unflawed politeness reminded Rinita of Prem Agarwal. But there were some marked differences as well, mainly in the confidence that came from unchallenged success. After the introduction, while the three of them got down to some budgeting work, Rinita, while sipping at the coffee offered to her, went around the room admiring the posters of the past blockbusters that had come out of the Dariyanani banner. Rinita had seen most of them on television, but without noting the name of the producer.

The meeting went on for one-and-a-half hours, but the expressions on Shahid and Munna's face did not reveal whether it went well or not. None spoke; Shahid climbed into an auto rickshaw and signalled the others to follow. Rinita broke the silence. "Where are we going?" she asked.

"To celebrate your success," came the expressionless reply from Shahid.

"Where?"

"Bombay Barbeque."

Three different outfits and as many different locations: sea-side, mountain-side and desert-side were where the dances were to take place. Rinita travelled with the cast and crew, under unmatched luxurious arrangements of an 'A' grade Bollywood banner to match steps with the diva Priyanka Chopra.

Though under tremendous tension so as not to invite a re-take for any failure of her performance, Rinita didn't fail to miss on the count of the number of times the camera pointed at her, though she would remain in the background.

At the end of pack-up, on her way back to Mumbai from Jodhpur via Delhi, Rinita dozed to a dream where she saw Priyanka sharing the same make-up room as her. And while wiping out the day's make-up from her chin with a tissue wet with some fragranced lotion, Priyanka congratulated her on a few steps which she confessed, she found better than her own.

Rinita had been on the tour for ten days which included extensive travel, long hours of shooting and even longer hours of practice. Before the travel, there were another fifteen days of elaborate practice and grooming sessions. These twenty-five days Rinita had almost remained out of touch with the rest of the world which included her best buddies in Mumbai – Shahid and company.

Twenty-five days isn't a long period, but what Rinita saw on her return prompted her to think otherwise. Shahid Khan, in contrast to his normal enthusiastic self, had become silent, jittery and prone to pessimism. He had also taken to occasional drinking, which he was never known to have been fond of. She also learnt from Munna, that Shahid and Fatima had been fighting more recently.

Rinita, too uncomfortable to talk to Shahid about it, tried to find out from Munna about the progress on Shahid's dream film venture. "I don't know much," Munna confessed. "Shahid-bhai does not take me to the meetings anymore."

"Why so?"

"I don't know. The last time I went was when you came along. That day Mr Dariyanani enquired about you. He asked Shahid-bhai a lot of questions about you. He praised your beauty…blah blah blah. Shahid-bhai tried to dodge his questions and get back to the project discussion, but every time Dariyanani reverted to talking about you. That day, the project discussion did not progress much. On our way back I asked Shahid-bhai why he got irritated when Dariyanani spoke about you. He gave me a very stern look which I did not understand. Maybe he was upset about the project getting delayed. Ever since, he has not asked me to come whenever he went to Dariyanani for a meeting."

"Are you sure they met again?"

"Yes, they did. He told me he was going."

Wrinkles appeared on Rinita's brow. She wondered what the matter could have been. That Shahid could not have been jealous of her she was sure. Maybe Munna was right about his project getting delayed which bothered him, or it was something completely different. Whatever it was, Rinita decided, she should try to find out herself.

The next time she was in the vicinity of Khar visiting another choreographer's office, Rinita dropped into Dariyanani's without any prior appointment. She found him exceptionally pleased to see her again.

"I was just passing by so I thought why not pay a visit to you," she said in a tone convincing enough to deceive Dariyanani.

"Very well thought, Rose. People like you make me feel important. It is necessary for a producer to have his office frequented by promising talents like you," he remarked believing that Rinita would fall for the flattery.

After some casual talk, Rinita brought up the subject of Shahid's project.

"So how is your discussion going on with Shahid about his project?" she enquired.

Dariyanani wasn't pleased with the change of subject, but he didn't make his displeasure apparent.

"Mr Khan is rather stubborn about a lot of things," he said. "I have given him some suggestions about how to make the project profitable, but he is not ready to accept."

"Like what, sir?"

"Call me Vasant," he objected.

Rinita had seen enough of old men to know their minds. She returned a smile, knowing well it was time she strengthened her guard.

"Like what Vasant?" she repeated the question only to comfort Dariyanani in revealing the truth.

"I told him to cast a popular superstar in the lead role, which he turned down. He said he has some theatre actor in mind. The superstar will not be able to get into the skin of the character he says."

"Is that all? I can try to convince him." Rinita needed to provoke Dariyanani to talk more.

Dariyanani pondered for a moment before continuing.

"I gave him a counter proposal which...kind of upset him."

"It would be his debut movie also, you know..." Rinita nodded to assure him she was all ears.

"And I will also be making a comeback after a few years. So I thought we should start off with a safer project. Once we are settled in, we should take up an ambitious project..."

"And what was the alternative proposal?" Rinita looked into his eyes.

"I wanted a long term relationship with Shahid. I was ready to enter into a three-film contract with him, but..."

Rinita remained unmoved, her expression didn't change a bit. She repeated Dariyanani's last word.

"But?"

"I wanted the first one to be a love story, *Salim Nabi Amar Rahe* to be the second one with all his terms and conditions...and the third we would decide through mutual discussion."

Rinita's eyes were fixed on Dariyanani's face, whose expression revealed he wasn't done yet.

"I thought he would be thrilled to learn that I wanted to launch you as the heroine in the love story. The hero wouldn't be a debutant, but any established star with an assured box office who would come at a reasonable price. Nice faces, pleasant songs and a predictable story – what else is required for a love story to be successful?"

Dariyanani ended with a question which wasn't to be answered. His expectation that Rinita would throw out her arms in jubilation on the prospect of an acting debut didn't come true, so he tried to push it further.

"I thought," he continued, "it was a win-win for all. All of you get a decent debut, and Shahid gets to experience his hands before taking up a bigger challenge. But the way he reacted..."

It was not that for a moment Rinita did not feel let down by Shahid, but she was not ready to believe that Shahid could have taken a decision out of jealousy for her. Either he was not ready to compromise any delay in his dream project or there must be something which Shahid thought wasn't right. Rinita had to find out more. She picked up her handbag and took leave from Dariyanani. "Thank you very much for sharing it all with me. I am grateful that you considered me without even knowing what I was capable of. I will talk to Shahid and try to bring about a change in decision."

"You will?"

Rinita leaned over Dariyanani's desk with her arms resting on the table and said flirtatiously, "Of course Mr Dariyanani...sorry Vasant. Who wouldn't want to be a heroine? I can't let it go so easily." Dariyanani caught a quick glimpse of Rinita's cleavage before she turned to leave the room.

Long after Rinita had left, Dariyanani rocked in his chair inside his empty office room, still smelling of Chanel No.5 left back by her.

"What a mess is this!" Rinita exclaimed with surprise at the plight of Shahid's room. Her early morning visit to Shahid's apartment had caught him unawares. He answered the door rubbing his eyes, still very much under the influence of sleep and previous night's alcohol. A couple of empty bottles of beer stood on the centre table. The manner in which clothes, books and papers were lying around was indicative of the fact that no woman (read Fatima) had rested her foot in the apartment for a good number of days.

Rinita went into the kitchen and made some black coffee. She returned to find Shahid looking reasonably fresh after a brush and a washed face, trying to put things back in place.

"Please care to have some coffee Mr Khan, and leave the cleaning to me," she said, to which Shahid complied without protest.

Shahid sipped the coffee. Rinita waited for the coffee to neutralize the hangover and once she thought it was fairly achieved, she initiated a discussion.

"We have not met since I returned," she said while getting into the cleaning act.

"Yes...actually I was a bit tied up," Shahid said apologetically. "So how did your shoot go?"

"Very good."

"Did you get a chance to talk to her...Priyanka?"

"Only once...one morning she happened to drop in at the coffee shop for breakfast. Just like her, I was at the counter picking up an omelette. She asked me whether I knew whether it was an egg white omelette or a full egg omelette."

Shahid laughed heartily. "So what did you reply?"

Rinita heart filled with joy to see Shahid laughing. "I said 'No idea'."

"You better have an idea next time," he said.

"I will," replied Rinita continuing to demonstrate obedience for her friend and guide.

An awkward silence followed.

"So, what about your project?" Rinita finally asked.

"Huh," Shahid made a strange sound and picked up the newspaper. "I don't think it will ever be made." Dejection was apparent in his voice. Rinita felt guilty, but no matter how bad Shahid felt talking about the subject, Rinita had to make him talk.

"Why? I thought your discussions with Mr Dariyanani were in the final stages."

"It was going, can't say going well. But then one day he said that he wanted me to do a love story for him which was fine with me...but then he said that he wanted that the love story should be done first, before Salim Nabi, which kind of alarmed me. If I had to do a love story or any commercial format for that matter, I could have done under the Chopra or Kapoor banner. I had such offers, but I chose to work with Dariyanani because I wanted to work on this particular project."

Shahid paused. Rinita wondered why he didn't mention that Dariyanani proposed to cast Rinita as the heroine. Was it that Shahid did not want Rinita to know so that she didn't feel bad about losing out on an opportunity? Or could it be that Dariyanani didn't mention her name to Shahid at all and he had made up that part of the story to impress her? Too many questions troubled her and she didn't have answers to any. Rinita knew she couldn't ask a direct question. She would have to find the answer from elsewhere, she thought.

"Hmm. So what are you going to do now? Talk to some other producers?" she asked.

"I am kind of fed up with this. I have purchased the rights from the author under the condition that if I cannot make the movie in five years, the right will be revoked and he will be free to sell it to somebody else. I still have four-and-a-half years left. I will go back to Kanpur, back to my theatre group and stage a play on this story. If I can catch the attention of the media, I will definitely find a producer."

"What the hell?" yelled Rinita "That will delay the whole thing by…god knows how many years. And what is the guarantee that it will succeed? And why not in Mumbai? Why Kanpur?"

"There is no guarantee of anything Rose, but one cannot give up. Kanpur will be much cheaper for a theatre production. There I had a theatre group which I can revive with lesser effort than starting one here."

"I am sorry Shahid, but I think it will be a backward step for you."

"It is, but momentarily, and strategically. I will return, and return stronger." Shahid's eyes became brighter, burning with confidence and conviction.

Rinita knew it was futile contradicting him, but she felt some comfort upon learning that Shahid wasn't quitting; he had a plan – a fairly achievable one."

By the time Rinita came out of the large white gate of RK Studio, it had begun to get dark. It was the first time Rinita had entered a film studio as a professional. The last few times she visited such a place was during her acting school days as a student on a study tour. The movie in which she made her debut as a dancer was entirely shot outdoors in the midst of nature. The tricks of taking the light, of following the lines drawn on the floor, of offering the best profile to the camera – all that she had learnt at school of indoor-acting was yet to be put to test. The audition for which she had come early in the morning and had spent the whole day watching hundreds of struggling actors like herself queuing up for one opportunity, had to be cut short because of 'lack of time'. In reality, the reason was a turnout of an exceedingly high number of participants as compared to what the infrastructure could have supported. Thus Rinita, along with most others, had to remain content with submitting a copy of her resume and photograph and an assurance of a call back if shortlisted.

Rinita didn't mind the struggle. She knew that things weren't going to be easy. In her assessment she was better looking than most of the other girls, also an imposing personality. The only aspect in which she thought she lagged slightly behind her counterparts was her language skills – both Hindi and English. But that she was working with on Shahid anyway. Thinking of Shahid, Rinita went back to her thoughts on Shahid's project. The auto rickshaw she had taken to reach Dadar from Chembur got stuck at Sion circle. It had started getting hot and humid.

One equation was yet to tally from both sides. If Shahid had a workable plan which he had shared with Rinita somewhat enthusiastically, why then was he so upset that he had to take to drinking? Rinita visualized a broken Shahid in his disorderly apartment. But why was the apartment in such a condition? It had always been neat, tidy and orderly. Fatima always kept a vigilant eye on the well-being of the place. The effort she took…wait a minute… Rinita's thoughts got intercepted with pertinent cross questions. Did it mean that Fatima wasn't around at the time when Shahid was in need of her so badly? Did it imply that everything wasn't well between the two? She had to find out the answers as soon as possible. She had barely touched her mobile to make a call to Munna when the phone rang. Mahesh's number flashed on the screen.

Rinita felt a mixed feeling of surprise, annoyance and affection, all at the same time.

"Hi Mahesh, after a long time…what made you call?" she asked accepting the call.

"Hi Rinita, how are you? You do not call me at all."

The allegation was expected. She had planned that she would surrender an apology and make some excuse, but she wouldn't reveal the real reason – which was the fear of her number falling into the hands of Arindam, a fear that still haunted her.

But fortunately it was Mahesh, who didn't need an apology to smoothen the conversation.

"Souvik showed me a film clip which our Mumbai entertainment bureau had sent in. They had shot the clip at a Priyanka Chopra shoot. We could recognize you in the background…you were in a red lehenga, weren't you?" Mahesh's voice reflected the ecstasy of the discovery and the inquisitiveness of how she had managed to get there.

Rinita felt worried. She knew it wasn't a conducive situation for her that she could be recognized by people she intended to keep away from. As if Mahesh knew what she would ask next, he continued, "But Souvik used his influence to edit your portion out. I was angry with him at first for doing so, but he explained to me that it would be unfair to show you kind of blurred in the background. He said we should wait for your full frame debut."

Rinita's lungs exhaled a good amount of air trapped inside. She could never repay Souvik's debt, she thought. The one wrongdoing he had committed upon her must have been washed away in the books of god by the numerous actions of friendliness and cooperation.

"I am so thankful to both of you, for your sweet thoughts and wishes," she said out of gratitude. "I hope you have not told anybody about it."

"Souvik asked me not to, so I didn't. Plus, you know I don't have many friends here."

Rinita felt sorry at his last words, but on a selfish note, she thought, it suited her perfectly. She said in a flirtatious tone, "Why do you need other friends? You have me, don't you?"

Mahesh, as expected, fell for her charm. "I know I do not need anybody else. I am just waiting for you to return, when we can marry and live together," he said.

Rinita, as she did always, believing what was the imagination of a juvenile mind said, "Of course dear, we will."

Rinita groped for the watch under the pillow. In the faint light of the night lamp, she read the hands of the watch pointing to two in the morning. Two hours had passed since she had climbed into bed, but except for the first half hour, when she dozed off rather fiercely out of a hard days' exhaustion, she had practically remained awake. The thoughts interrupted by the phone call rushed in again. The thoughts that things were not too well between Shahid and Fatima saddened her. She had to know the reason, and try too, if anything was within her capacity, to get them back together.

After the action point was identified, Rinita decided it was time to catch some sleep. A stray question, however, which hadn't occured earlier niggled in her mind – how had they get hold of her Mumbai number? She had been careful enough not to share it with any of her Kolkata connections, including Souvik.

Rinita knew it must be Souvik, and not Mahesh, who could have cracked it, but how and from what source. She typed a message on her mobile and dispatched it to Souvik's number, expecting a reply message or a call back sometime next day. But to her surprise, in five minutes, her phone beeped. It read: *'Employed RTC Mumbai reporter to track the girl in the pic. Full confidentiality ensured. Don't worry'*.

Rinita had guessed something on similar lines. Her eyelids were heavy with overdue sleep, but because it would look rude to end the conversation at that, she wrote back, *'Why are you awake at this hour?'* This time the message came in in less than one minute – *'Because you are still awake. Kidding;) Night duty. Good night. Catch u later.'*

Rinita smiled, then slid the mobile under her pillow and closed her eyes.

◆

The next day, Rinita called Munna at the Borivali coffee shop where the four of them has spent some good times together.

"Yes, it is true," he confessed.

"But why?"

"Lots of things. I don't know it all." Munna played with the coffee mug, waiting for it to lose some of the heat. He felt uncomfortable to look into Rinita's eyes while talking about such things.

"Tell me what you know."

"Shahid's plan was not received well by Fatima's family. Apparently they want the marriage to take place this year, but the way things are going, they are not sure that it will happen soon enough, if at all."

"If at all? What does *that* mean?" Rinita almost shrieked.

Munna got nervous at Rinita's violent reaction. "Why are you yelling at me? I am just quoting what her father had said."

"I am sorry. I got upset. What does Fatima have to say?"

"She wept, and protested, but when her father said that 'You are free to marry him against our wishes. Go ahead if you have to', she looked at Shahid with teary eyes but took a step back."

"Oh no, that means Shahid went to her place?"

"Yes, he went there with a taxi waiting...asked her to come with him if she loved him."

"And she turned him down?"

Munna chose to remain silent; the answer was already known.

"But why?" Rinita asked in desperation.

Munna shook his head.

Rinita felt miserable imagining what Shahid must have gone through, and at the same time guilty as Dariyanani's change of mind had happened after seeing her.

But Shahid was a brave man and he was firm in his goal. It would be a crime not to try to do something, she thought.

"So much happened in such a short time and you didn't tell me. I was away for just three weeks; it feels like such a long time. And I spoke to you over the phone. All you said was 'everything is fine'," Rinita took out some of her frustration on Munna.

"Shahid-bhai asked me not to tell you anything. It was your first assignment and you did not deserve any distraction, he said."

Rinita's remorse aggravated. Her respect for Shahid, if there was some room still left, would have expanded. A true mentor, she thought.

◆

Over the next two days, as there weren't any auditions or appointments, Rinita chose to stay indoors. She had by then learnt by experience that aimless wandering in the film and studio localities wouldn't fetch her work. The search for work had to be rather focused and pointed. Also, the heat and the sun wasn't good for the skin.

The few things she did over those two days were to visit a local cyber café and search for any material on Vasant Dariyanani. She asked a few friends and acquaintances in the film world, whom she had met in the course of her auditions and assignments, to share whatever information they could find on Dariyanani.

All that she could collect in two days, when put together, made a fairly interesting read:

Dariyanani had inherited the diamond export business from his father who passed away when he was still a student. He dropped out of college to take control of the business. While at school and college, he took a fancy for films and expressed to his father his wish to become an actor, which was turned down without any consideration. The untimely demise of his father and the responsibility of the family took the film-ghost out of his head for some years. But after ten years, by the time the business and the family had settled and the ghost resurfaced, Dariyanani had lost much of his prime, and his dreams of becoming an actor was replaced, upon advice of some well-wishers, with that of a producer.

So Dariyanani became a producer in the eighties, and during the decade, produced ten blockbusters. His love for glamour surpassed his love for business and in due course, as an outcome of consistent neglect, the diamond business collapsed, and Dariyanani became incapable of producing any more films.

His rumoured affair with a struggling actress (who appeared in a couple of his movies) died as fast as his business, and Dariyanani went out of the news.

Recently, having sold off a lot of ancestral property in a prime location in Mumbai, Dariyanani had made a good amount of money and re-entered Bollywood under a new banner. His wife and daughter were known to have abandoned him for reasons not known, but guessed to be property related.

The most interesting information was saved for the last: that Dariyanani in recent years had been living with a lady who was half his age and had been his daughter's governess.

Quite an interesting character, this Dariyanani, Rinita wondered dropping the dossier on her bedside table. Whatever she had to infer about Dariyanani lay within the pages she had just read. There was no time to unearth more. Rinita picked up the phone and dialled Munna to check when Shahid was planning to pack his bags.

"You will have to convince him to stay back for another fortnight...somehow," she told Munna in an authoritative tone. Rinita had to rely on Munna on this front, as she had neither the courage nor the strength to face Shahid, because she knew Shahid would never approve of her ways of mending things.

The last call of the day went to Dariyanani's office; her request for an appointment was granted.

◆

The appointment was post-lunch, which gave Rinita ample time to spend in the beauty parlour where she got her hair trimmed, eyelashes curled, a manicure and a pedicure with a fresh coat of nail polish; she chose a deep red shade which contrasted well with her fair complexion.

At home she wrapped a sari – white chiffon – the translucent, fine and slippery material stuck to her body highlighting the perfect contours to a beholder's delight. The carefully draped sari hid under its mysterious folds the revealing sleeveless blouse, with a knot at the back. After applying matching lipstick and eyeshadow and a judicious spray of Chanel No. 5, Rinita stepped out of the house and into the radio taxi.

That Rinita had wanted to visit him alone had prompted Dariyanani to advise his secretary to cancel all other appointments before and after. Dariyanani wore a silk pyjama-kurta instead of his trademark half-sleeved shirt thrown over the old fashioned pleated trousers. He liked the fragrance left behind by Rinita the other day, so despite a famed miser that he had become, shelled out nine thousand rupees for a Chanel No. 5 for himself (though later expressed displeasure at the size of the bottle which came at that price).

Rinita reached fifteen minutes ahead of the schedule, which gave her the time she needed to run a quick scan through herself in the washroom mirror. She pressed the bindi, ran her hands through the hair to adjust the locks and patted a tissue on the lips.

A wait of fifteen minutes for Dariyanani, after having heard that she was in, was a bit too much to handle. He sprayed the Chanel in calculated quantities, adjusted the flowers on his desk, admired himself in the tiny pocket mirror hidden inside his drawer, and ran his hand over the few strands of hair still standing on his head. But fifteen minutes would not pass. So he stood and went up to the door, opened and peeped outside.

"Hi Vasant."

He heard her voice come from the opposite direction than the one he was checking.

"Oh Miss Rose. Please come in." Dariyanani did not know how he spoke those words. His eyes popped out at what he saw and his heart beat faster than what his physician would have permitted.

"You look so smart in this attire," Rinita commenced her mission. Dariyanani blushed like a boy just fallen in love.

Dariyanani took his turn in flattery, leaving nothing out of his list of admiration – from Rinita's earrings to the straps of her high heels.

Once the initial emotion had settled, Rinita contemplated it was time to get down to business.

"Vasant, the reason I am here..." Rinita started in a serious note, making Dariyanani feel an unknown nervousness.

"I have thought, and re-thought and re-re-thought about your proposal to us...but somehow a win-win formula didn't come out. Shahid doesn't want anything else but his dream project to be his debut movie. He is ready to get back to Kanpur and stage a play on the script, but not do any other film," she continued keeping a close eye on Dariyanani's changing expressions.

"You know," she continued, "I am in some kind of a commitment with him...professionally, as he had been my mentor and guide since I came to Mumbai. He has offered me the role of Kirti in the play and I cannot say no."

Dariyanani's mouth made a small opening, through which all his dreams seemed to escape. He never expected the meeting to start with such a negative pitch.

"So..." Rinita paused to give some space to Dariyanani to vent his astonishment.

"So what?" he asked, his mouth still open.

"We are busy packing bags, and settling rent agreements."

"Oh no Miss Rose, you cannot do this. You have such a brilliant career waiting for you here. A director can start his career later, but for a heroine, it's always a race against time!"

"Can't help it, Vasant. Not that I don't know all that. But a commitment is a commitment..."

Rinita cast a sad look towards the corner of the room where pictures of Hindu gods were put up, as if to say, 'if only god had destined otherwise'.

Dariyanani followed her eyes.

Neither spoke for some time, both looking equally sad and out of hope, until Dariyanani said, "Isn't there any possibility of a... of a..."

"Compromise?" Rinita filled in with the word she was waiting to hear.

"Ah...I mean, sort of..."

"I have an idea, if you would agree..." she said cautiously, testing the waters.

"What?" Dariyanani looked curious.

"If you would agree to do *Salim Nabi Amar Rahe* first, then I can convince Shahid to enter into a three-film contract with you. The second once would be a love story of your choice, and the third one can be decided later after discussion."

"But..."

"As a package deal," Rinita interrupted Dariyanani, "I will also sign a three-film deal with you."

Rinita noted a sparkle in Dariyanani's eyes. She continued with more vigour. "None of us will work in any project outside your banner until the three movies or expiry of five years, whichever is earlier, is over."

Dariyanani crossed his fingers and put them against his lips in a gesture of serious thought. Rinita stared at him so strongly that Dariyanani felt intimidated. He looked in a different direction and spoke, "But Miss Rose, you are not getting the point. I do not have anything against Shahid's script; it is only that I cannot risk my money at this stage. I want to earn something before I take that risk."

"I fully understand, Vasant. Because you were out of the industry for some time, you want to play safe. I hope you understand the benefits of having an award-winning movie in your portfolio." Rinita tried to reason him into her proposal.

"I know all that, but the project is way too expensive for an art movie." Dariyanani's shrugged his shoulders; Rinita knew he was right.

"I am not saying you do not look at profit. All I am saying is do not look at the profitability of each project in isolation; rather, look at the profitability of the three project package."

Realizing that Dariyanani was still unconvinced, Rinita dropped the bomb. "And you think about the ancillary benefits... you get me with the deal."

"Get you?" Dariyanani had placed his foot inside the trap.

"I mean...get to work with me." Rinita pretended as if it was an innocent error on word usage.

"Oh," Dariyanani rode a see-saw of hope and despair. "I do not have that much money to invest in two successive films," he uttered faintly in a sad voice.

"Oh, you don't need your own money to make a film these days, Vasant. Sorry to say, but you are clearly out of touch with the modern financing mechanisms."

Rinita's knowledge of modern film financing system was based on what she had read in film magazines, but she pretended to be wiser otherwise.

"There are corporates running with sacks of money after production houses that have a brilliant idea and could execute the production with their money. It would be a joint production with your house being the executive producers and theirs the financers."

Dariyanani shook his head to signify that he knew all that Rinita had just said. "They don't run after out-of-the-market veterans like me. They prefer people with a good record or younger people with no record. I do not stand a chance."

Rinita realized that Dariyanani wasn't an easy customer; he had studied the market well.

"Have you ever thought about why Shahid has not found a single producer before me? Because his project is a difficult one... not only about the expenses, but about the political message, it directly points at partisan politics. Such movies do not attract a universal audience."

Rinita knew Dariyanani's points were valid; also that if Dariyanani turned down Shahid, it would need a miracle for him to find another producer, no matter how much media attention his play would draw. Not only would his career be in jeopardy, his personal life would be in ruins too. No matter how brave a face Shahid had put up, his drinking and his messed up apartment had exposed his fragility.

Rinita noticed that Dariyanani's arms were rested on the table. Her logics were failing; it was time to shift to plan B.

Rinita clutched Dariyanani's hands with both her hands suddenly. To do this, she had to lean some distance forward on the wide table separating both of them. "Don't tell me there isn't a way out of this. You cannot break my heart like this," she said looking deeply into his eyes.

Dariyanani was overwhelmed with the unexpected touch of soft young female skin. He looked down. Rinita's newly made up nails reflected a part of his face. Dariyanani made no effort to remove his hand. With a lot of shyness, he somehow managed to look back into Rinita's eyes; his heart virtually came out of his chest at what he saw.

Rinita waited for the time when Dariyanani would look up, and once he did, she shrugged her left shoulder with calculated precision, just enough to let the pallu slip and fall partly on her lap and partly on the floor, thus exposing her full breasts. Her blouse had a deep cut, and did the rest of the work.

Dariyanani felt he was having a heart attack – sweat appeared on his face and neck, and goose-bumps on his hands and some portion of the chest and stomach. His throat felt dry and scratchy, and inside his chest a feeling of breathlessness.

Rinita could notice the sweat and certain other external changes which confirmed that the medicine had started to work.

"Vasant, you can't do this to me, can you?" she implored.

Dariyanani did not know what to say. His brain wasn't working, and his eyes refused to move away from the protruding flesh. An organ in the lower part of his body felt harder.

"Please Vasant, say something." Rinita knew every passing minute could diminish the effect of the magic. Once his brain would start working, material logic could surpass other emotions. If Dariyanani had to commit to something against his calculated prudence, it had to be right there and then.

Dariyanani felt an increased pressure on his head to say something – something which would not result in a withdrawal of Rinita's hands and the covering of breasts.

"I can try...if you help me," he replied with a lot of difficulty. His tongue became heavy and wouldn't move with normal effort.

"I will do whatever it takes. Please find a solution."

Rinita's open assurance was enough of an impetus for a wild commitment. "I think I can find a financer."

Rinita was woken up by a short vibration on her mobile. She rolled over to face the other side and pulled up her sheet, but on second thought decided to see who it was. What she saw startled her. It was a message from Dariyanani asking her to meet him at his residence in the evening. She was asked to come in the same sari that she had worn to his office the day before. The address of the Khar apartment detailed up to the block and flat number was included.

Rinita was pleased that the initial leg was successfully accomplished – the mouse had hit the trap. But an unknown fear also bothered her. The success of her mission rested on how well she could execute the final stage. Good that he had mentioned the dress in which he wished to see her; a tricky decision didn't have to be made.

Dariyanani, dressed in a dressing gown, answered the doorbell. His hair was wet from a bath. Rinita offered a warm smile and a bottle of white wine wrapped in fancy paper.

"Very thoughtful, Miss Rose. The more I see you, the more I am amazed. Please come in." An expression to match his words flashed on his face.

Over the next one hour, they finished off the wine, talking about some things from her past and certain things from his, both conscious not to reveal too much.

Dariyanani had not taken the trouble to get into regular clothes, knowing well that whatever he would wear ultimately needed to be shed. Rinita too, being loyal to her designs, didn't mind this minor impoliteness from an otherwise well behaved man.

"I hope you don't have a double thought about the proposal," Dariyanani said fastening the belt of his gown while still on his march.

"Not at all."

Dariyanani came up to Rinita and looked into her eyes, seeking a verification of her words from her expression. Rinita made eye contact, the determination was evident.

Satisfied with what he saw, Dariyanani rested the burning cigarette on the ashtray, loosened the belt and slid the gown off his shoulders. He stood before Rinita, dressed only in a trunk. The otherwise lean body carried some flab around the waist. The fair non-hairy chest must have appealed to a lot of women when this man was younger, Rinita thought.

She rose up to stand in front of him and placed her hand on his chest. Dariyanani removed her hand; evidently he wanted to be the one in charge. He slid the pallu off her shoulders, exposing her blouse, and tucked his finger inside it to feel the breasts. Once he reached the nipples, he paused, withdrew his hand and reached out for the knot at the back with both hands circled around her. He untied the knot and let the blouse drop at her feet. There was no surprise on his face to see Rinita's full breasts lying open in front of him, as if he knew that she wasn't wearing a bra. He gently pressed both her breasts with both hands, kissed them and sucked them. When Rinita reached out for his trunk, he violently removed her hands away.

After a good amount of sucking and kissing and caressing, he threw her back on the sofa. Rinita was taken aback at this action, but different people approach sex in different style, she thought and waited for Dariyanani's style of love-making.

Dariyanani unrobed the rest of Rinita's clothing and sat down on the sofa beside her, caressing her thighs, passing his finger over her vaginal opening again and again. He kissed her lips, passionately reaching out for the tongue. While the lips were locked, his hands slid up from the thigh back again to her breasts. This time he pressed the breasts so hard that it hurt her. Had her mouth not been locked in the kiss, she would have screamed. Gradually his hands left the breasts and moved up to her neck. Dariyanani caressed the neck for some time and then pressed it hard with both hands, as if he wanted to strangle her. It suffocated Rinita. She applied all her strength to free herself from Dariyanani's clutches. She pushed him back with both hands, scratched him with her nails and bit his lips with her teeth.

Dariyanani eased his hands and removed his mouth. Rinita could see his eyes had become red; a fearful expression of anger reflected on his face.

Rinita had never seen a man become so wild in bed. But before she could organize her defense, Dariyanani clutched her by her hair. "You bitch, you whore...you think you can overpower me? Show me how much strength you have!" He yelled.

Rinita felt like her hair would tear off. She continued desperately scratching Dariyanani with her nails, and noticed with some solace that it had caused some bleeding at places. But that was too little an effort to defeat Dariyanani. The man, she realized, was surprisingly strong.

Dariyanani's torturous means weren't over. He picked up the cigarette and pressed the burning end against her breast. Rinita cried out in pain.

Rinita could take it no more. She groped for her handbag which she had left somewhere on the sofa on her left. Rinita managed to reach out to the purse, she knew exactly which pocket to dig in; her fingers touched cold metal.

Rinita shut her eyes before drawing her hand in full force right across Dariyanani's chest, allowing the sharp edge of the Victorinox Swiss knife to cause whatever damage it could.

The cut must have been a deep one, though unlikely for a tiny weapon like the Victorinox, or perhaps the trauma of a possible injury caused a mental defeat for Dariyanani, as he released his grip and withdrew from Rinita's body in a sudden impulse.

"You stabbed me...you stabbed me..." Dariyanani murmured frantically, holding his chest which bled profusely. "Oh my god... somebody help me...I will die..." Dariyanani continued like a mad man, though his voice was so feeble that it hardly went out of the room which was shut from all sides. As blood continued to gush out, his face turned pale. His hands started to shiver and he dropped on the floor.

Rinita took full advantage of the opportunity. She wore her clothes, picked up her handbag and rushed towards the door. At the door, she turned back to take a final look at Dariyanani. He lay unconscious on the floor; his chest bore a long cut at two places. Blood flowed in multiple streams across his chest and onto the floor.

Rinita knew she had to leave if she had to escape any further trouble. But Dariyanani lay helpless and bleeding. If nobody attended him, he may very well die, she thought. She needed to do something to prevent any permanent damage. She looked around the room and found Dariyanani's mobile lying on the dining table. She went up to it and searched the address book for 'Mohato'. She had heard Dariyanani calling his secretary by that name. Mohato appeared and she typed 'HELP' before pressing the send button.

All the way back, in the taxi, she thought of what she had just survived and a cold shiver ran down her spine. But by the end of the journey, another thought bothered her – what if Dariyanani, out of unbearable pain, got a heart attack? The police would definitely find her out and put her on trial.

◆

Rinita could not sleep that night. The fear of anything fatal happening to Dariyanani bothered her more than the consequences of her name getting entangled in a scandal, or a criminal case, or both.

Rinita remained indoors the whole of next day, thinking about all of that and more without any conclusion. She even dialled, the landline number at Dariyanani's office, but received no reply, which worried her even more. She hardly felt hungry and survived the day with two glasses of juice, a lassi and a sandwich. The day came to a close and another night passed in sleeplessness. But towards dawn, Rinita's eyelids became too heavy to remain open, and she fell asleep.

Her eyes opened close to noon by a short vibration of the mobile. An sms had come. She also saw two missed calls from Shahid within a span of five minutes. The message was also from him, it said: *'Mr Dariyanani has agreed to produce Salim Nabi Amar Rahe. He wants to book the floors for September. Busy days ahead. Will talk later.'*

Rinita jumped up in surprise and joy; her fatigue and tension had vanished. She felt a biting sensation from the inside of her stomach – she was hungry. The message effectively meant that

Dariyanani was alive and recovering. But she could not believe what she read. Why had Dariyanani taken this decision she wondered. Was he afraid that Rinita would blackmail him or go to the police?

She called Shahid back, but as his phone was busy, she wrote back *'Congratulations'*.

Rinita managed to speak to Munna over the phone; he sounded ecstatic. "Shahid-bhai is almost running like a mad man from one place to another finalizing his cast, crew and logistics. You know, Mr Dariyanani wants to start the shoot as early as September. September is lucky for him, he said," he said in one breath.

Munna had supplied her with all the information and confirmation she had been seeking. But there was one last question. "Does Fatima know?" she asked.

"I assume yes," Munna said after a quick thought, "because Shahid-bhai said he will be going over to her place for dinner tonight."

Rinita felt relieved. She thanked god for putting the pieces together.

In the evening, Rinita went out for a walk. For two whole days she had remained confined to the four walls of her room, in anxiety and fear of an unknown danger. The fear was so fierce that she almost forgot about the burn on her breast which had started to heal on its own. She walked alone in the falling light of the dusk along the pavement inhaling the open air. On her return after her aimless wandering she found she had a visitor waiting for her in the sitting room.

"Mr Mohato? What brings you here?" she asked him; the anxiety returning to her face.

"Miss Rose, it's assuring to find you in good health." The guest smiled pleasantly at her.

Fifteen minutes later, as that was the time it took to walk down to the nearest coffee shop, Dariyanani's secretary revealed the purpose of his visit.

"Mr Dariyanani is extremely apologetic for what happened that night," he said.

Rinita, at the beginning felt rather uncomfortable at the fact that what had transpired between her and Dariyanani that night was known to a third person, but it was she who had messaged him that night.

"Both of us realize that it was you who saved his life that night, despite such a traumatic humiliation," he continued.

Rinita went on stirring the coffee.

Mohato got slightly concerned at no change in expression on Rinita's face as if either she did not hear what had been said or she did not choose to attach any importance to it.

"Are you with me, Miss Rose?" he expressed his desperation to be heard seriously.

"Yes, I am."

"He is thankful to you for saving his life," he repeated with a conviction of extracting a reaction out of her.

"Why are you emphasizing on the 'saving his life' thing, it was only a scratch by a pen knife!" She objected.

"Maybe...but a lot of blood was lost...and the doctor said a few more hours of inattention could have been fatal...and he has a heart condition as well."

"Then he should not have done such a thing." Rinita's words were sharp and piercing, without any signs of weakness or emotion.

"That is exactly why I have come to you."

Rinita looked up to meet Mohato's eye. She waited to hear more.

Satisfied that he had her full attention, Mohato resumed. "Mr Dariyanani married quite late in his life. Mrs Dariyanani was ten years younger to him. While Mr Dariyanani got involved in film glamour, his wife got involved with his friend. One day he caught his wife and his friend in a compromising situation in his own bedroom. He went mad with fury and beat her up very badly. Their daughter protested the violence without knowing the cause and got a fair share of the beating as well. Both his wife and daughter left him. There was a police case and a scandal. But as Mr Dariyanani had good contacts, he managed to influence the police and the press, and soon the matter was hushed up. Since then, till today, his wife and daughter live separately."

Mohato sipped his coffee. Rinita wondered why she was being told all this. There was absolutely no connection between this story and that night's incidence, she thought.

Mohato read her expression.

"Since then Mr Dariyanani has lost all trust in women. He believes all women are unfaithful and has been, or will be adulterous at some point in their lives. He started behaving strangely. He won many partners, mostly aspiring actresses; he tortured all of them. He visited brothels but there again did the same. He says that whenever he is in sexual proximity with any lady, he is reminded of the infidelity of his wife, he loses his senses, becomes violent and does what he did with you."

Mohato paused and sipped his coffee.

"Hmm..."

Mohato looked at her, expecting to hear something.

"But I heard he has a steady partner, some lady who was his daughter's governess. How does he manage that relationship?" she asked.

"She is a childless widow. She has willingly accepted the torture. It has become a kind of job for her, out of which she earns a livelihood and security for the rest of her life."

"By being beaten up?" Rinita asked in disbelief.

"There are always takers of many things if you have money," he said.

"Hmm..." Rinita made the sound again, this time to indicate that she agreed.

"I hope you will forgive him?" Mohato returned to where he started from.

"Was the cut really deep?"

"Unevenly deep at two places, otherwise only a scratch... but there was a lot of bleeding and chances of a heart attack."

"He should not come close to women at all. Everyone will not buy this reasoning, even it was true."

Mohato's face shrunk. Was it that Rinita was planning legal action? Would she go to the police? Dariyanani had sent him to pacify her and he could not fail, he thought.

"He agrees with you. But as any normal human being, he at times gets attracted beyond control…like in this case."

"Hmm…"

Mohato's constant threading of the forgiveness line made things rather clear to Rinita. She understood that Dariyanani did not want a police case against him at a time when he was reinventing his career and that is why he agreed to produce Shahid's dream project. There was no harm in pardoning him, she thought, especially when the purpose had been fulfilled.

"I am sorry to hear all that, Mr Mohato. I wish Mr Dariyanani a swift recovery. Also please pass on my thanks for agreeing to produce the dream project of my friend Shahid." Rinita turned to the waiter and called for the bill, bringing down the curtain on the discussion.

One year flew by rather quickly with a lot happening around Rinita and her small world. Shahid's ambitious project sailed rather smoothly. Minor troubles with government authorities with permissions to shoot at high security zones could be overcome with a little persuasion and a little political influence. Shahid had offered Rinita the role of Karla in *Salim Nabi Amar Rahe* – a small but important character who gets Salim and his love interest Kirti together, which she played rather convincingly.

In an effort to ease up things with Rinita, Dariyanani offered her an item song in a small budget murder mystery which he produced alongside *Salim Nabi Amar Rahe* with another director. Rinita found it rather amusing that Dariyanani should spend that much money as he did in roping in the most expensive composer and choreographer for her song, which was also the only song in the movie. Rinita came to know from Mohato who also reviewed the finances that more than a quarter of the budget of the movie was spent on that single song. Kind of repentance? she wondered, but didn't bother to express either pleasure or displeasure at the special treatment.

The Priyanka Chopra movie had released during Christmas holidays and had been a runaway success. Rinita went to theatres with Shahid, Munna and Fatima to watch the movie in which she could be seen for about forty-five seconds, dancing with and around the superstar. Forty-five seconds in a five minute song is remarkably substantial, observed Shahid. Despite being in the background and slightly out of focus, Rinita could easily be recognized as the most important person in the frame beside the lead actress. "Was the DOP (Director of Photography) in love with you that he gave you such prominence?" teased Fatima for which she got a friendly pinch on her forearm from Rinita.

Shahid and Fatima, after the launch of the *Salim Nabi Amar Rahe* had become formally and officially engaged in a small family ceremony in Kanpur where Fatima's family flew down to meet Shahid's. Their marriage would be held, as agreed mutually between the two families, after the release of the movie.

Rinita received calls from Souvik and Mahesh congratulating her on her debut, and from Chaitali and Abhishek who complained about not being told and what they happened to discover while watching the paid preview in a London theatre. Chaitali also shared the big news from her side – that she was five months pregnant. It dug up a forgotten sorrow in Rinita – of having lost a child her womb had warmed for some time.

Around March, a two-minute edited version of the flamboyantly shot item number was released on YouTube and it went viral in no time. The catchy tune, erotic choreography and Rinita in a revealing bar dancer costume won more than a million hits in less than a week's time. Miss Rose became a popular name among young male filmgoers who didn't mind a small sexual tickle here and there as a part of 'paisa-vasool' formulae. The sudden unanticipated publicity made Rinita alias Rose into a frontrunner contender for similar item numbers with other production houses.

'Unanticipated but not unplanned' was what she had learnt, first from Shahid and then from Mohato, who confirmed that the leak was made on purpose to grab the attention of potential financers who would invest in Dariyanani's ventures as Dariyanani's own finances were fast depleting.

"He is using me to raise funds?" Rinita asked Shahid with some displeasure.

"Nothing wrong, Rose...we all are commodities. We will live as long as we sell, and you should be proud that you are selling well." Shahid's explanation removed all doubts from Rinita's mind and she started enjoying her success. Soon, she signed an item number contract with one of the top three banners in commercial film making in India – a massive, massive leap was how Rinita described the opportunity to one of her roommates, overcoming the dilemma she had faced before accepting the offer.

"Should I continue doing item numbers? Wouldn't I be labelled as an item number girl?" she asked Shahid, as she always did, for advice.

"Had Shah Rukh Khan thought the same way, he would not have done television, and then he would not have been Shah Rukh Khan."

The big banner song was to be shot in a London studio. Why should an item song which would feature an Indian and was to be shot indoors had to be shot in London was beyond Rinita's comprehension. Big banners had big budgets and therefore big reasons to do small things in a big way, she thought and concentrated on getting a passport. And in one month's time, she was standing on the Westminster Bridge, zooming her new twenty megapixel camera at the Big Ben.

❧

The seven-day schedule involved a gruelling work regime which stretched well into extended evenings. One full day was allocated to local sight-seeing arranged for the entire group. Rinita would have preferred to spend that day with Chaitali, who asserted instead that Rinita should tour the city with the group as she was stuck at home, taking care of the new born. It would be unwise to return home without having seen the city, she insisted. Rinita accepted Chaitali's argument promising to spend the last day of the shoot which was bound to wrap up by the afternoon with them at their Kings Cross residence.

The shoot went perfectly as planned. The flight to Mumbai wouldn't take off till next afternoon, which gave Rinita little less than one whole day to spend with her friend in London.

Rinita shared the post code with the black cab driver and was taken to the spot without any difficulty. On her way, Rinita picked up a cotton nappy set from Tesco, some flowers and a bottle of wine from Marks & Spencer. One hundred pounds was a decent amount to be spent on gifts for her special friend and family, she contented counting the change.

Being a Friday, Abhishek was back from work early, and Chaitali was at home attending to the child. They spent the evening together, discussing various things of common interest and learning certain things and ways about the film industry. Only once for a short while, the discussion became awkward when Abhishek, having caught a glimpse of the diamond ring on Rinita's finger asked, "Why did you and Priyanshu split up? You two made such a lovely couple. I see you are still wearing the ring."

"Come on Abhi," Chaitali intervened, "personal matters are personal matters…let's not pry." And there ended the subject.

Rinita and Abhishek emptied the bottle; Chaitali excused herself as she was breastfeeding her son. One bottle didn't seem to be enough for Abhishek who uncorked another from the cellar. The first one they toasted to Abhirup, their son, and the second one to Rinita's upcoming stardom. The Indian dinner cooked by Chaitali was polished off by Rinita. The taste of home-cooked Bengali food, something she had not had since she had left Souvik's home where his mother used to cook for pregnant Rinita, delighted her and she showered Chaitali with hearty praises.

Rinita helped Chaitali with the dishes while Abhishek ran a quick check on his mails. By the time the dishes were done, the day's light peeping in through the splits of the blind had started to fade. Chaitali had to retire to bed for a bedtime feed to Abhirup and another night of intermittent sleep.

"With a baby around, you forget your normal sleeping cycle," she said. Her words had exhaustion wrapped around them, but no traces of complaint.

"It is a happy thing for a mother to do…you will understand when you will have one," she said before leaving her to Abhishek's hospitality. Rinita hoped her words would come true someday.

Abhishek, as a dutiful host, showed Rinita the guest room and the attached washroom. "All yours for the night," he said "but I am sure you are not going to sleep right now."

"Definitely not, I can't sleep until it is dark at least." Rinita said pointing at the window through which a decent amount of light came in and flooded the bed.

"Great, then let's finish the second bottle. But in case you want to change into a more comfortable outfit, feel free to pull something out of the wardrobe. Your friend's size will fit you well." Abhishek showed her the wardrobe he was talking about.

"Oh, thank you. I will, she told me. But for the time being I am fine."

They returned to the sitting room and made themselves comfortable in the heavily cushioned perpendicularly arranged sofa set.

Abhishek poured the wine and absorbed all that Rinita knew about celebrity lifestyles, especially of the glamorous ladies – which locality they lived in in Mumbai, how big were their apartments and how expensive were their cars. She also told him all she knew about the link-up stories often published in the film magazines and tabloids and how true they were.

"I never thought that men could be so inquisitive about Bollywood gossip," she couldn't resist observing on a light note.

"I don't know why you say so, because I see all my male friends profoundly interested in such things."

"Maybe because they are away from home and Bollywood is the easiest culture-connect."

"Could be, but how does knowledge about a top heroine's lingerie brand connect me culturally to my homeland?" Abhishek said smiling animatedly.

Abhishek's lingerie remark, though not completely out of context, made Rinita uncomfortable and conscious of Chaitali's absence. She decided she would not drink beyond the glass she held, which she was halfway through.

Abhishek finished his glass and refilled it. He offered Rinita, who politely refused.

"You want to see yourself? I have your songs on a drive. Chaitali and I watch them often." Abhishek pulled out a pen drive from a drawer of the television cabinet without even waiting for Rinita to approve. "Here it is." He flashed the drive with a wide smile.

Rinita, not wanting to be rude to a self-proclaimed fan of hers, nodded.

The forty-eight-inch LED first played the Priyanka Chopra song followed by the leaked item number. Abhishek nodded his head in rhythm with the songs in childlike enthusiasm which somewhat amused Rinita.

The two minute video was neatly edited, making room for all the titillating sequences and steps. In the song, Rinita played a bar dancer dressed in a brightly coloured traditional Indian ghagra-choli styled and modified enough to eroticize the package. At one point a drunken customer was seen tempted by her inviting and provocative gestures, dance up to her and pull her translucent mirror-studded dupatta in an attempt to peep into the blouse, whom Rinita then pushed away in a rhythmic movement.

Abhishek played the video for the second time, this time pausing it at the point when the man pulled the dupatta. He turned to Rinita with a mischievous smile. "What would you do if someone really did that to you?" he asked.

Rinita found the question rather strange and silly. She felt slightly edgy but recovered quickly. "No one would do that with me. I do not work in a cheap bar like what is shown in the video. I deal with educated and respectable people," she said in a bid to warn Abhishek against any further impertinence.

"Who said educated people don't get titillated? Don't they have the same things like everybody else?" he argued.

"But they would conduct themselves more dignifiedly in public," Rinita came up with a counter justification.

But Abhishek was not in a mood for any theoretical discussion on morality. He moved closer to Rinita and in a flash pulled her pallu off her shoulders to expose her cleavage held tightly inside the blouse. "Don't you think I am educated?" he said with a grin as if taking pride in what he had done.

"What are you doing? Have you gone mad?" Rinita cried out, protesting the outrageous behaviour, placing both her hands across her breasts.

"Come on, Rose. Be game. I know you don't have middle class inhibitions," he tried to force her hands away to get a full view of the bulging breasts.

"Please Abhishek, get back to your senses." She struggled to keep him away.

"Come on bitch, don't be a saint now. I know how many you have fucked on your way up." Abhishek's face deformed with anger; refusal wasn't an acceptable option for him.

Rinita could not take it any longer. Her respect for the host and her best friend's husband had depreciated. She pushed Abhishek with all her might. Surprisingly, overpowering Abhishek wasn't as difficult as she thought it would be, may be because intoxication had deprived him of a lot of his natural power. Abhishek's grip loosened and his body flung to the other part of the sofa, and Rinita ran inside the guest room and shut the door. She tried to lock it from inside, but the British locking system was rather new for her and she couldn't make it work within a reasonable time - that is the time by which Abhishek had recovered and followed her. She left the door in despair and rushed into the attached washroom. Fortunately, the washroom had, along with a typical British lock, a traditional latch and bolt, which she shut from inside.

Abhishek closed the guest room door behind so that minimum sound would leak into the master bedroom where Chaitali was sleeping with their son. He felt like banging the bathroom door, but decide against it. He tapped the door gently instead. "Rose, I beg of you. Please sleep with me for once. I have been starving for months with a carrying wife and a new born. Please help me," he pleaded.

"Please stop all this nonsense Abhishek. You have gone mad. I am not going to listen to any of your crap anymore. I am not going to open this door for you."

"Come on dear. You can't stay there all night. You will have to come out. Give me a chance. I promise I will give you a lot of pleasure. Don't worry about my drunkenness. I am at my best when drunk."

"Just shut up and leave me alone," Rinita screamed in disgust.

Abhishek banged the door for some more time, and pleaded, and eventually passed out on the guest room bed.

Not hearing any sound for some time, Rinita guessed Abhishek might have passed out, but she could not be sure. He could have been pretending, she thought. So she decided to remain inside until the morning. But then what would happen if Chaitali was to see her in that situation? Either her family would break up or she would take sides with her husband and blame Rinita for making inappropriate advances on her husband – both equally unwanted and undeserving for her lovely friend, she thought.

Sitting on the floor, resting her back against the wall of the bathtub, she thought and thought hard about the most appropriate step to take. She decided to leave before morning; because night time was not safe for any woman to venture out in an unknown city, she decided to wait till dawn.

It was the best night in many ways for Chaitali. The baby did not cry out hungry too many times, allowing her to catch a good sleep. In the morning, she woke up Abhishek in the guest room and asked about Rinita. It was concurred by both that she might have left early in the morning for some urgent reason, not choosing to spoil the sleep of her hosts. Both Abhishek and Chaitali tried to contact her over phone to wish a safe flight, but in vain.

It did not occur to Chaitali to ask Abhishek what he was doing on the bed meant for Rinita.

A few days after Rinita's return from London, Shahid and his crew had to fly down to Himachal Pradesh to shoot a very critical portion of *Salim Nabi Amar Rahe*. The sequence in which the Defence Minister of India goes out on an aerial survey of the India-Pakistan line of control at Siachen glacier and finds himself in Pakistani territory. This sequence, for Shahid, was the most challenging in technical as well as logistical terms. The ten-day schedule in Himachal, which was chosen for its similarity in landscape with the ordinarily inaccessible and tension-torn Kashmir, gave Rinita the much-needed opportunity to spend some time on her own.

She had finished shooting for all that was on her plate, so she decided to take a few days off to recover mentally from the crude shock inflicted upon her from unexpected quarters. Since the night of the incident in London, there had not been a single moment when she was awake that the dreadful incident did not haunt her. She flipped through some of the pictures on her mobile photo gallery. The one clicked on the night of their marriage reception showed an innocent smiling Abhishek, and the one taken at the Glenary's, Darjeeling presented a warm loving expression. Was there some jealousy in his eyes when the snap at Windamere was taken the day after Priyanshu had presented Rinita with the ring? Rinita did not know at that time; she didn't know even now. Was it the sexual starvation due to a pregnant wife or the provocative dance number that had caused the momentary insanity? Whatever it might have been, it wasn't the most envious of situations to be in.

On the penultimate day of the Himachal outdoor shoot, Mohato joined the team with pay cheques and some paperwork for the authorities. That night, having completed a very demanding schedule, a relaxed Shahid sat for a round of drinks with Munna and Mohato in his hotel room. Mohato had carried a bottle of scotch from Mumbai which he uncorked. Shahid, however, settled for his favourite beer supplied by the hotel bar. After two rounds of whisky and an equivalent quantity of beer had vanished, Munna asked Mohato a naïve question. "It is still a mystery to us how Dariyanani changed his mind and gave a green signal to the project. Do you have any idea, Mr Mohato?" he asked.

Mohato remained silent for some time, as if in a dilemma whether to take the question or to dodge it wisely. But when Shahid joined Munna in the query, he sort of enjoyed a position of prominence – a position of someone in possession of insider information, which nobody else had the privilege of being privy to. He acceded to the persuasion and in a semi-intoxicated state narrated what was decided between him and Dariyanani to remain as a closely guarded secret.

By the time Mohato had finished his drink and also the revelation, Shahid's face had turned stiff, his eyes blood red. The effect of alcohol had lost its effect on him when he proclaimed, "If what you are saying is true, Mr Mohato, I am walking out of the project right here right now."

Munna was equally shocked but his mind, as it was, being less creative than Shahid's and therefore more practical, produced counter arguments for why such a rash decision should not be taken. Mohato's position was the most precarious. It didn't take long for him to realize the potential damage he had caused to several persons and the project. He therefore joined Munna in his effort to salvage whatever remained to be rescued.

The ramifications of the leaked video and the news of breaking into an A-list production as an item girl could be felt in Mumbai too with Rinita starting to receive a lot of attention and a decent recognition of her name. All kinds of offers poured in – interview for a moderately successful vernacular film magazine, ribbon cutting at a dance school inauguration, being a judge at children's dance completion, and performing a solo in a star-studded stage show. Rinita could feel that people in the local trains and on the streets could recognize her, point at her and talk in low voices amongst themselves. No matter what they spoke, the matter that Rose had become a distinctly recognizable face among the thousands and millions in the crowd was a matter of pride for her, as would have been for any performing artist. But Rinita could not find a friend around her with whom the happiness could be shared. Shahid had already denounced the project and had not spoken to her since. Munna had to follow the footsteps of his master. Her roommates, though nice on the face, burnt with envy from inside. Souvik was too far and too busy for a meaningful chat. And between her and Chaitali, after the London incident, a tall invisible wall had come up.

Rinita called up Mahesh and told him all that she wanted to tell her friends about the nicer things happening in her life, and Mahesh was blindly encouraging and genuinely happy, like always.

Dariyanani got half mad at the shelving of *Salim Nabi Amar Rahe* – half because he still got his financial calculations right. He preponed the release of the murder mystery to Navratri in September that year, from the originally slated Diwali, to book some immediate profit so that some loans could be paid off and some interest cost saved.

Mohato was on the receiving end of some chosen words of 'appreciation' from Dariyanani, who out of gratitude for him for saving his life held back from showing him the door.

The doldrums in Shahid's career took a toll on his personal life as well when Fatima's family pressed for calling off of their engagement. Fortunately, unlike previous time, Fatima stood strong and voiced her decision to go ahead with the marriage without considering what the future would have in store for them. And defying family orders on both sides, Shahid and Fatima got married much earlier than planned. Fatima, however, looking at a devastated Shahid could not comprehend why he should take such a reckless decision. Why should he have any reason to be upset if Rinita had on her own accord traded her body for the project? Who knows, she must have had her own interest; after all, she bagged the meaty role of Karla, she thought. If one reason for Fatima's hurrying into a marriage was to comfort Shahid at a time of difficulty, the other reason was suspicion that Shahid had developed an emotional leaning towards Rinita. Why else should he get so damned upset that he should sacrifice success which was lying on a platter to be grabbed? That bitch was out to chew Shahid's head; one positive fallout of the fiasco was that she was out of his head, Fatima comforted herself.

Rinita chose a pinkish-red anarkali salwar with a gorgeous brocade border to walk the red carpet at the premier of the murder mystery at the prestigious Metro Big Cinema at Dhobighat, Mumbai. Flashbulbs clicked when she made her appearance along the cast of the movie, which did not have a female lead, and she, with her item song, was the only glamour quotient. The premier was graced by the presence of Bollywood bigwigs and ended in liberal applause at the intelligently conceptualized movie and the phenomenally crafted bar dance number. The commoners in the audience seemed to be more interested to catch the first glimpse of the complete version of the super hit leak rather than the thrill of the mystery. Rinita had the rare privilege of signing the most number of autographs that evening and being the subject of most number of photos.

Dariyanani, visibly encouraged by the general response to the movie guarded her from the inquisitive press and took her in his personal vehicle to the Taj Lands End in Bandra West where the after-premier-party party was organized.

Towards the end of the party, which flaunted the best of cuisines and alcoholic beverages, when the crowd had started to lighten, Dariyanani came up to Rinita to check whether everything was fine with her.

"Absolutely fantastic," she said in delight, "but could you please arrange for a car to drop me at my place? It is well past midnight," she asked and observed with some concern.

"Of course, all the arrangements are in place. But before you leave, I want you to meet someone who has become a big fan of yours." Dariyanani said in a low voice, tapping gently on her back with his hand.

"Who is it? Is he in the party?"

"He is, but not here, in a room on another floor. He is the financer of the movie. It is because of him that we are seeing this day. If you can make him happy, only sky is the limit," he said and winked mischievously.

Rinita took no time in reading the signal. "But Vasant," she said in a desperate attempt to escape the situation, "I am having my periods…" Her heart beat fast with anxiety; sweat appeared on her brow; her fingers trembled at the anticipation of another forthcoming nightmare.

"Oh do not worry, Ayub Hussein is a very considerate person. He will not cause you any harm. After all, he is an admirer. I thought you never had inhibitions or pretentions, am I wrong?" Dariyanani cunningly floated the name of the financer, a name he knew would scare her.

Rinita, like anybody living and working in Mumbai, knew who Ayub Hussein was. Very few in the Mumbai film and business circles had missed an extortion notice from this notorious underworld don, who in recent times, controlled his empire from the comforts and safety of Dubai.

Rinita understood that there was no escape. The reputation that she had built for herself was out to hit back at her. But she knew she wasn't the first Bollywood casualty picked up to warm his bed, and if the law enforcers continued to label him as permanently and untraceably absconding as they did, she wouldn't be the last too. But she had to make a try, as she did on several occasions in the past, to find a way out of the adverse.

"Can't we meet later...after a few days...by when this thing is over?" she asked Dariyanani in a frantic voice.

Dariyanani shook his head. "He is off to Dubai tomorrow and will not be back in six months. But do not worry...I told you, he is considerate."

"Well, in that case will you please allow me to use the washroom? I want to clean myself up before going to him." Rinita sounded down and depressed as if all her hopes were lost.

Dariyanani appreciated the idea; it was a rational request in this situation, he thought, and positioning himself as a guard outside the women's washroom, allowing Rinita five minutes to do whatever she needed.

With five minutes and the clock ticking, Rinita locked herself inside a commode cabin and dialled, with trembling fingers, Shahid's mobile number. Shahid was the only person she believed who would, if required, risk his life to come to her rescue. Once, twice and thrice Rinita called frantically, but there was no reply.

With quarter to four minutes gone, Rinita gave up her last hope. It was an unjustified expectation, she thought, that a newly wedded couple would be awake to take calls at that hour of the night.

Rinita stepped out of the cabin and stood in front of the giant mirror behind a row of wash basins to take a final look at herself. She looked at herself like how a shepherd would look at his herd before they were taken away for slaughter. But no, she wouldn't pity herself. It was a grave she had carefully and meticulously dug for herself over the years. "Goodbye," she told her reflection in the mirror and walked out of the washroom seven seconds before the five minutes would expire.

Fatima waited for the phone kept on silent mode to stop flashing Rinita's name before she would delete the entries from the missed call list and switch it off for good. The phone which lay at the centre between a widely awake her and her snoring husband would carry no evidence of Rinita's calls for any future reference.

Abu Hussein indeed did justice to his reputation of being a considerate person. Being a man of few words, he did not waste time in acclimatizing Rinita before the butchering. But he made it a point to use a condom to comfort her and protect hygiene on the other. He also, as a mark of generosity at the special physical condition, offered to penetrate the anus instead of the normal organ. "No bleeding there, I suppose," he said, laughing his heart out. But even after ten minutes of intense struggle, when he could not put his big thing through the virgin opening at the rear, he resorted to normality in the most widely used normal physical position of man on top. Brutal power on the top of the victim, as it has been for ages, penetrated for seven long minutes the profusely bleeding and stinking opening between the parting of Rinita's stretched legs. Rinita bit her lips tightly to hold her pain from giving away, loosened her legs and the muscles inside the vagina to allow the savage accomplish with ease whatever he demanded.

Around ten in the evening Mahesh returned from work to his apartment. He pushed the key inside the keyhole and twisted it. He noticed a silhouette seated on the staircase which ran into the floor above. Ten o'clock on a rainy night with no other soul in close proximity was a good enough setting for a scary situation. But Mahesh wasn't like any other normal person. Living alone for years in a cruel city with a disability had taught him to be brave and strong.

Mahesh turned towards the human being seated two steps higher than his landing, wrapped in a shawl in a way that nothing including the face could be seen.

"Hey, who are you?" he asked.

The person made a small opening around the face and looked up at him.

"Rini!" he exclaimed catching sight of the pale face and red eyes. The previous night's eyeliner and mascara appeared smeared. Her hair, whatever could be seen from the little opening was disorderly. She shivered out of cold or fever or both.

"What a surprise? How are you here?" he asked realizing something wasn't right.

"I went to your old place, the hostel where you lived. They told me that you do not live there anymore and that you have asked your mails to be redirected to this address," she said slowly in a feeble voice, taking deep breaths between words.

"Please come in, you look sick."

Mahesh helped her get inside. From the touch of her skin he could feel she was running a high fever.

Rinita looked around the decently decorated room which was evidently the living room because it did not have a bed.

"Nice work," she said in what sounded like a murmur.

"What, this flat? Souvik arranged this for me. The guys over there were not very kind, you see. He said, what will you do with your money? Who do you save for? Instead live well, live with dignity," Mahesh said while getting a glass of water for his guest.

"True, thank you," she said gulping the water like she had been thirsty for ages.

"You don't have any luggage?"

"I have nothing."

"You look sick. I think you need to stay here for the night. And you need a doctor."

"Would you mind if I stay here for longer?"

"If you were the same Rini, you would not have asked," he said pretending to be stern.

Rinita smiled. "I want to get back to being the same Rini I had left behind."

"Then you lie down on my bed while I cook some dinner for us and let me call the doctor," he said with such authority that Rinita found it amusing.

"Boil me some instant soup and give me a Paracetamol if you have. And I don't need a doctor. I will recover in a few days on my own." No matter how matured Mahesh had become, to Rinita he was still the little Mahesh whom she could order.

"You think I still live on bread and Maggi?" Mahesh asked as he pulled out a blanket from his cupboard while Rinita positioned herself on Mahesh's bed.

"Wrong," he continued, "I have learnt to cook well enough to satisfy my taste buds."

"Good for you," Rinita said covering her shivering body.

Hot chicken corn soup, two slices of bread and a 'Parasafe 500' was what Rinita had for dinner. One hour after having fallen asleep, Rinita in a natural response removed the blanket from her body; the fever had left her body, causing a lot of sweat. Rinita wanted the fan to be switched on. She looked at Mahesh sleeping like a child on the makeshift bed he made for himself on the floor. She hesitated to wake him up, though she knew the fan would have comforted him more; nor did she have the strength to lift herself to the switchboard. They both suffered the heat, but slept well in an unknown comfort of being with each other after what seemed like ages.

◆

Rinita woke up to find three faces leaning onto her from three corners of the bed: Mahesh, Souvik and another middle-aged man with neatly combed hair and a thick moustache. Rinita guessed he must be a doctor.

"What is the time?" she asked looking at the window brightly lit from outside.

"Half past ten," replied Souvik. "How are you?"

"Better…"

"What happened?"

"Long story."

Souvik understood that she wasn't in a mood to discuss. "This is Dr Partha Pratim Sen and here is your beautiful patient," Souvik undertook to get the introductions done instead. "You are perfectly safe in his hands."

"Well I did not need a doctor…but since you insist, let me talk to him in private," Rinita said looking at Souvik and Mahesh by turns.

Both left the room.

Dr Sen pulled up a stool and leaning further towards Rinita asked, "Do you have a cold?"

Rinita silently looked into his face for some time deliberating whether she should or should not reveal the truth to the doctor.

"The fever is due to sudden mental shock," she said. "I had a similar fever in the past when I had seen a cobra."

"And what did you see this time?" asked the doctor.

"A man."

Seeing Dr Sen fold his brow trying to guess what that should mean, she clarified turning her face in a direction away from him. "It was a forced sexual assault, doctor."

Dr Sen stood momentarily dumbfounded before being rescued into a conversation by Rinita.

"I had my periods running at that time...even now for that matter. He entered me from the back and then from the front causing some injury to both the passages. I feel intermittent burning sensation in both the places. The backside is paining so much that I cannot lie with my back against the bed for long," Rinita explained the problem with so much clarity and conviction that Dr Sen felt embarrassed

"You are no older than my daughter, I salute your spirit," he said.

Rinita did not react; the kind words meant nothing to her.

Rinita didn't hide anything from Souvik too. She left it to his wisdom as to how and to what extent he should reveal the truth to Mahesh.

She did not know what Souvik had told Mahesh, but she noticed Mahesh had become more sensitive and caring. After three days in Mahesh's den under strict supervision and meticulous nursing, she felt better, though her wounds were still far from healing. Ointments had to be applied to secret places where her hands wouldn't reach. Mahesh offered to hire a nurse, but Rinita thought if so many men had touched her and she had not complained, why not Mahesh with his natural innocence! She did not for once feel intimidated exposing her secret organs to her childhood friend and eternal admirer.

Mahesh had taken a long leave from work, Souvik used to drop in whenever he was free before or after work. The two of them took turns in cheering her up.

"I want to spend a few days in Phoolbari," Rinita said sipping some tea during one such cheering up session.

Souvik and Mahesh exchanged glances, wondering whether it was possible.

Mahesh tried his best to dissuade her, citing practical logistical problems. Neither his nor Rinita's house was available for living, and there were no decent hotels too.

But Rinita wouldn't relent. "I want to spend lazy afternoons by the banks of the Ganga watching the ferry sail against the tide," she said.

"Let's do something," Souvik came up with an idea. "I know a house by the Ganga in Bally...similar landscape as Phoolbari... well maintained with all modern amenities. They lend the house for picnics and marriages. We can hire it for as long as we want."

"Wow," Rinita jumped up in joy. Her face glowed with hope and happiness. "Let's do that. Money will not be a problem," she said.

◆

The two-storied white building was a river-bank private property that came with well furnished rooms, a fully functional kitchen, a personal lawn leading to the bank, and a host of caretakers ready to carry out orders. Bally, like Phoolbari, lay on the western bank of the Ganga. "The sun will wake me up...just like it did in my little home in Phoolbari," Rinita observed gladly while surveying the house.

Mahesh and Rinita checked into the house with their luggage, while Souvik promised to pay them regular visits. Rinita got all her stuff sent across to her from Mumbai.

One week in Bally and Rinita had recovered fully, but Mahesh was in no mood to treat her as such. He continued the nursing while Rinita enjoyed every bit of extra attention she received from her friend.

"I miss throwing stones into the river," Rinita exclaimed one afternoon sitting with Mahesh under a shady tree in the lawn, watching the ferry. "Can't we go there…at least for some time… when it's dark?" she asked.

Few boys jumped into the water from a nearby ghat and swam haphazardly celebrating their moment of freedom.

"Just like us, isn't it?" Rinita asked watching them.

"Let me ask Souvik if he could drive us there." Mahesh could not ignore Rinita's passion of reliving the sweeter memories of the past.

"Thank you Mahesh, you are a darling," Rinita planted a gentle kiss on Mahesh's cheek.

"When do we go?"

"Do we have a poornima coming up anytime soon?"

"I saw a Bengali calendar in one of the rooms. Perhaps one of the marriage parties left it behind. I will check it out."

◆

Mahesh offered his hand which Rinita needed to climb the steep steps leading to the elevated platform of the Shiva temple. The steps had broken down completely. It was the first time she needed help to get there.

Past midnight, the round silver moon was right on top of the river, casting its spell on every big and small thing it touched. The breeze wetted by the water carried the smell of rain pouring somewhere not very far away. The lights at the bank on the other side cast a long streak on the water sporadically broken by the waves.

"Here you are." Mahesh's words broke the spell on a mesmerized Rinita. She turned to find a handful of pebbles lying in Mahesh's palms held together into a bowl.

"Ah...are you a mind reader?" she asked. Mahesh smiled shyly at the compliment.

"You know Souvik, the favourite sport for the three of us was to throw pebbles from here far into the water...would you like to try?"

The three of them emptied all the pebbles Mahesh had in his stock into the water - some went far, some fell near, but none failed to emit its share of joy.

Two hours flew by recollecting the memorable incidents associated with the temple. On the way back, the three of them walked down silently up to the house in which Rinita had lived with her mother. The house, in which new tenants were living, had received a new coat of cheap exterior paint. The narrow space in front, in which Rinita's mother used to grow vegetables and flowers, had been cemented and fitted with a railing.

Three shadows stood silently for some time as if paying homage to a sad event. Rinita wiped a teardrop.

◆

Chaitali applied last minute touches to Rinita's make-up, straightened the pleats of her dark red zardosi Benarasi. The crown made of white tuberoses stitched with a thin wire was placed on her head, from which the gold tikli seemed to have emerged to rest on her forehead.

A traditional high ceilinged palace with thick pillars and arched doorways was liberally decorated with fancy lights and seasonal flowers. Lots of guests had come wearing the best of outfits and the warmest of smiles.

At the traditional custom of *shubho dristi* where four of her friends, including Souvik, Shahid and two others, held the board in the air on which she balanced herself fearfully in a cross-legged posture; holding a pair of betel leaves with both hands held together to cover her eyes.

The time had come when the betel leaves had to be parted so that the two pairs of eyes, of the bride and the groom, could meet. The crowd cheered; the elderly passed naughty jokes.

Rinita's heart beat faster with an unknown excitement. Never in her life did she feel that shy to do something which was so common and natural. She was a performer who could act and dance in front of hundreds of people, but at her wedding, she evidently wasn't her natural self. Was it customary to be shy on their wedding day for even the smartest of girls, she wondered.

'Ting-ting' the sound of a spoon hitting against a cup and Mahesh's voice came at the same time, "Wake up dear Rini, tea is ready."

Rinita opened her eyes to see Mahesh with a steaming cup of tea, standing beside her bed in a position which had, since Rinita had come over, became a routine for him.

Realizing that it was a dream which had got interrupted by Mahesh's untimely wake up call, Rinita sat up on the bed, trying to assimilating what she had seen. Did she see the face of the man she was getting married to? No, she did not, she was sure. It was at the nick of time when the betel leaves were about to be parted enough that she woke up.

"What is the matter?" he asked noticing a difference in her expression.

"Nothing, just a dream."

"A good one?" Mahesh handed over her cup and sipped from his.

"Very good one." Rinita took the first sip.

"Do you remember?"

"Clearly."

"What was it?"

"I was getting married," she said and watched Mahesh's expression change into a serious and concerned one.

"With whom?" he asked rather unwillingly.

Rinita took some time to get mentally ready to say what she had decided to.

"You," she said decisively.

Mahesh couldn't believe his ears. He needed to hear it once more, but was scared that he might hear it right this time – some name which wasn't his. He wished the world could end there and then, so that Rinita wouldn't get to revoke what she had just said, even if it was spoken by mistake.

"Who?" he asked in a feeble voice to secure a reconfirmation.

"You, Mahesh…you! Who will ever love me the way you do?"

"Do you really think no one can love you more than him," asked Souvik looking at the water from the edge of the lawn from where the slope ran down sharply into the river.

"Are you jealous?" Rinita asked, making it quite evident that her answer was a 'yes'.

Souvik smiled but did not reply. He wasn't a saint that he would stay immune to her charm, especially when she was back, and so close.

"Do you think he will be able to satisfy all your needs?"

"What needs, Souvik? Physical, or emotional, or both? Mahesh loves me since when I wasn't what you see. He had seen me slipping and slipping, but never withdrew his hand. He will love me even when I will lose all my beauty, all my success, when my skin will wrinkle, my hair will turn grey and thin."

Both fell silent when Mahesh came in with freshly fried fish fingers. Rinita sent him back for a bottle of water.

"I need your support Souvik, even if you are jealous."

Souvik overcame his feeling – a faint hope which he had nurtured unconsciously all along. He smiled with watery eyes. "I am only too happy for both of you," he made himself say.

◆

Not many people knew about the low key wedding between a hot emerging starlet and her childhood companion. Souvik made all the arrangements, whatever minimal was necessary, under strict confidentiality. The crackling sound of currency notes freshly picked up from the ATM convinced the marriage registrar that putting up a backdated notice on a board affixed on a damp wall in a dark corner outside his office wouldn't cause any harm to any person involved or not involved in the marriage in any manner. The signings on a few copies of light green court paper and a fat register signifying 'coming together of four hands' – a common Bengali idiom used to indicate union through marriage – got accomplished. Everything, from the garlands the newly-weds would exchange after the signing to the witnesses were arranged by Souvik; he himself and Mr Gupta, the cafeteria man from RTC whose job Rinita had once saved did the honours.

Rinita had foregone most of that. She, like any other young girl of her age, had dreamt of as uncompromisable three things: a dark red zardosi benarasi, a platinum wedding band and the Hindu ritual of '*saptapadi*' – the seven rounds around the pious fire while the priest recites the mantras spelling out seven vows for the couple to follow, one for each round.

The night before the signing, Rinita slipped off the diamond ring for the first time since Priyanshu had put it on. A lot of pictures from the days at Wellington, some pleasant some spiteful flashed across the sparkling diamond. Rinita put away the ring in a safe compartment inside her wardrobe. The ring, out of constant wearing left a white mark on her finger; the mark, she thought kept alive the memories of Priyanshu safely in a secret compartment inside her heart.

At the same time, in another part of the city, Souvik was trying a mobile number – once, twice, multiple times, only to find it switched off. In despair, he tried a landline number which went on ringing without an answer.

'I had made a deliberate attempt all these days not to live up to the promise I made to Priyanshu: that I would inform him as soon as I got to hear something about Rinita. Not sure whether, by now, he has seen Rose's videos on YouTube and has recognized her. But today, I have tried hard to fulfill my promise in vain. Whose misfortune is it – his, Rinita's or mine perhaps will never be known,' he told himself, dropping the phone on the table out of despair.

Priyanshu had managed to trace Souvik's number from the call list of Rinita's office's landline telephone and contacted him in an desperate attempt to get some information which could lead him to her, but Souvik having declined to oblige made a promise which he never intended to honour. Some compelling force inside him made him dial Priyanshu's number on the eve of the most important day of Rinita's life.

On the day of the wedding, in the late evening, before the auspicious spell ended, the pious fire was lit on the raised platform of the abandoned Shiva temple in Phoolbari village by the priest. Rinita and Mahesh completed seven rounds of the saptapadi. The temple and the river which had been witness to all that was good in their lives, along with the holy fire, stood witness to a marriage uneven in some ways, but more than even in many.

Epilogue

Rinita Bose alias ROSE

"Let me get some coffee." Souvik rose to his feet. He looked at the grim faces of others by turns – Priyanshu, Abhishek and Shahid. The clock had struck twelve. It was almost lunch time, but none of them felt hungry. Priyanshu's was the only head which moved in the affirmative. Shahid said, "I'd rather go out for a smoke." Abhishek nodded his head at Shahid.

"Well, in that case, I'll also join you. I am expecting a parcel to be delivered to me anytime now," said Souvik, thus leaving Priyanshu with little choice to do otherwise.

Four of them moved out of the lounge at the Apollo hospital and headed for the main entrance, leaving behind Mahesh who was the only person, being the closest kin, to be allowed in the operation theatre waiting area.

Chaitali was in the hospital in the morning when the doctors came in to deliver the first briefing. Being a woman and a mother, Chaitali was best suited to understand the significance of what the doctor had said.

It was an ectopic pregnancy, they said, which went unnoticed due to persistent bleeding, which made it look as if the menstrual periods had not been skipped. When asked, Mahesh had confirmed that she had at times complained of abdominal pains. What happened the previous night was an emergency situation of 'collapse' – the rupture of the fallopian tube. An immediate surgery required to remove the tube was performed to perfection, though the fetus was not in a condition to be replanted into the uterus.

Just when the audience prepared to heave a sigh of relief that the worst was over, the doctors came up with more – Rinita had suffered a heart attack during the operation. "She must have had a heart condition which went untreated for years," they said.

What that meant was that the danger had flipped departments – from gynaecology to cardiology – but remained hanging over Rinita's head. The doctors prepared for a longer, more complex emergency coronary surgery.

Chaitali, scared and tensed and sad, asked the doctors about the chances. "Fair, but not certain," came the reply.

While the men settled down for a smoke, an RTC staff arrived with a bouquet of freshly arranged roses pinned with a letter. Souvik plucked out the piece of paper and unfolded it to read.

"What is that?" asked Priyanshu.

"A note from a bastard. I don't want Rinita to read any shit which upsets her while she recovers. Let me see what the bastard has written.

Rinita,

Eight months after we last met, I got the news that my wife was pregnant with my child. But the baby did not survive to call me Daddy. Maybe the gods paid me back for my sins. Though of no consequence, and of little solace, please accept my sincere apologies for all the sins I had met out to you. I am really sorry. If possible, forgive me. May god bless you.

Arindam

Souvik read it aloud.

"Who is this Arindam? Must have done something really bad," said Shahid.

Souvik nodded, but didn't reply.

"I also have something to confess. Though unknowingly, I have also caused her a lot of pain. I think I should also write a note to her," Priyanshu observed.

"Me too," said Abhishek taking a cue from Priyanshu.

"I will also write something." This time it was Shahid.

Soon, a wring pad and some envelopes were procured from a local stationery store.

Dear Rinita,

I was told you traded our love for money, and reluctantly, I had to believe it, until one day when Joydeep and Dad fell apart and Joydeep tendered his papers at Wellington. Maybe out of repentance or a compelling urge to hurt my father, he told me all that had happened at Wellington in my absence. Dad does not live with us anymore. He doesn't have the face to stand in front of me and my mom. I think he is suffering enough. Please forgive him if you can.

P.S. By the way, you will be happy to know that I am also married, though not sure whether happily.

Yours,

Priyanshu

◆

Dear Rinita,

Chaitali still doesn't know what happened that night. And I do not know why it happened. Was I mad, or had a devil entered my mind? However, thank you for not ruining my marriage. Please forgive me.

Regards,

Abhishek

◆

My Dear Rose,

Every day when I wake up, I thank god for giving me you as a friend. You know how much my career is indebted to you? But what could I do in return? Fatima confessed much later that she saw your calls but didn't tell me. The little fool was jealous of you. But trust me, she did not imagine the calls were so important. The poor girl has repented enough. Please forgive her.

Your undeserving friend,

Shahid

◆

Dear Rinita,

My sins are no less than Arindam's. I have been his alibi on so many occasions, but never did it hit me back so hard. It is your generosity that you have treated me as your friend. What I have done for you later is only a part repayment of what I owe.

Please forgive me dear.

Souvik

◆

All the letters, even Arindam's, were put inside separate envelopes and sealed. They returned to the waiting hall where Hemant, arriving after a long journey, was searching for some known faces.

"We have written letters to her. Do you want to write something?" Priyanshu asked him.

Dear Rinita,

We now have a two-storied school building with the best library in the district. Our school has won an affiliation from the State Secondary Board. The hospital now has ten beds with a full time medical officer, and two nurses. We also treat patients from nearby gardens and villages.

We all miss you. Please visit the garden to see it all with your own eyes.

Recover soon.

Hemant

◆

Souvik went upstairs to hand over the letters to Mahesh so that they could be delivered to Rinita once she was out of the operation theatre.

Mahesh held the letters tightly against his chest with both hands, staring at the big clock ticking away, and waiting for the red light burning on top of the operating room door to switch off.

Did the doctors say 'fair, but uncertain' or 'fair and certain'? – Words jumbled up in his mind. A thin film of water washed the walls of his eye blurring his vision of the hands of the clock. A faint voice could be heard in a distance: 'Mine went further.' The voice echoed. The pebble thrown into the river had caused the water to spill; the ripples ran in all directions in circles.

◆

Postscript: Salim Nabi Amar Rahe *was later completed by Shahid Khan himself. It won the Rajiv Gandhi Award for National Integration, Best Screenplay award at the National Film Awards, the Best Debut Director at the Filmfare Awards and a special mention at the Cannes Film Festival.*